THE HERAKLION GAMBIT

A NICK TEMPLE FILE

JONATHAN DYER

CARTA

The Heraklion Gambit
A Nick Temple File
Copyright © 2013 by Jonathan Dyer

Designed by Coline LeConte

Carta books may be purchased for educational, business or sales promotional use. For information, contact Carta Studios LLC, P.O. Box 311, Sonoma, CA 95476

ISBN-13: 978-0-9899816-1-3
ISBN-10: 0-9899816-1-4

Library of Congress Control Number: 2013955984
Printed in the United States of America

To the Men and Women of
Field Station Berlin
1983 – 1986

CHAPTER 1

GAME ON
APRIL 30, 1955

The small harbor is an unlikely place for a Superpower showdown. Its crystal blue water, fragrant Mediterranean air, and slow moving, small fleet of tired fishing boats all combine to paint a portrait of daily, lazy tranquility. And here, life imitates art. As quiet as the days are, the nights are quieter still. A halyard slaps against a mast; wavelets splash quietly against the seawall; a few voices float across the night's warm breeze; a fisherman snores in the wheelhouse of his worn-out trawler; another peaceful, languid night is under way.

Nick Temple lies on a rooftop propped up on his elbows, his cheek pressed against the wooden stock of his M1C sniper rifle. He scans the southern end of Agioi Pantes–the Island of All Saints in Mirabello Bay off the coast of the small town of Agios Nikolaos–through the rifle's powerful M82 scope. He knows what started to accidentally reveal itself in Athens more than a year ago is going to end tonight, one way or the other, right here on Crete. He knows that a handful of men and women whose names and deeds will never appear in headlines or history books will have one chance in the next few hours to thwart a southern thrust that has been a Russian dream for centuries. And if by some miracle all the pieces fall into place and the gathering Soviet storm is stopped, he knows that once the dust settles and the bodies are counted his career as a charter member of the CIA and his marriage of 16 years will both be on life support. The career he might be able to save; the marriage, not a chance. And he has no one but himself to blame. Blaming Vanessa would be easy. He could blame her careless beauty, or her cool sensuality, or her limber morality. He stuck around when he should have walked away, when she left the door open, and tomorrow he's going to pay for it, big time. But tonight he has a job to do. If there is a tomorrow, it'll have to wait.

A flash of light on the north side of Agioi Pantes tells Nick zero hour is here. He can just make out the signalman's silhouette through his scope. Another flash of light. The silhouette hasn't moved. Nick has one shot, one chance. "Picking off Greek Commies. A helluva way to make a living," Nick thinks to himself. Or, as Bob Arnold said when he heard about the chance to end the matter before it got started, "Shooting the Paul Revere of the Greek Communist Non-Revolution Revolution." Taking out the signalman is his last chance to let the Soviets know they've lost the element of surprise. He'll know in a matter of minutes if they got the message.

He exhales, waits, and squeezes. The crack of the rifle destroys the night's peace. A third flash of light instantly illuminates a dying man dropping to his knees moments before his lifeless body crashes face first onto the gentle, sandy slope of the Island of All Saints.

"Score one for Mika."

CHAPTER 2

HAPPY ANNIVERSARY
FOURTEEN MONTHS EARLIER

Nick Temple is usually at the office at least half an hour before his secretary. However, another late-night quarrel with his wife results in his having to drive their children to school to demonstrate his commitment to and involvement in his family's life. Nick knows the gesture is lost on his kids who would rather be chauffeured about in their mom's '54 Mercedes 180 than in their father's remarkably unexceptional black 1951 Fiat 1400. Their school on Berlin's Hüttenweg in the American Sector is just a few minutes from his Zehlendorf office, but the school's start time of 8:00 a.m. means Nick is running behind.

The office, such as it is, isn't much to look at from the outside. It sits in a large suburban Berlin house confiscated by the Americans from a Nazi who four days later saved the Allies the cost of a trial by committing suicide four years later than he should have. The rest of his family fled Berlin certain that the Soviet Army was everything Nazi propaganda had said it was. When the family showed up six months after the war claiming the house to be rightfully theirs, they were told to fill out a claim and that the Army would get back to them. That was eight years ago. Nick is reminded of their claim of right on a more or less annual basis when some family member who drew the short straw shows up to serve another worthless court document on the house's current occupants, employees of the Central Intelligence Agency. Nick's reaction is always the same.

"Life's a bitch, and then you die."

The two-story, late 19th century structure is set back about 30 feet from the street. A low, wrought-iron fence covered by several coats of black paint separates the front yard from the sidewalk, and a crushed stoned path leads to the small set of wooden stairs that take the rare visitor up to the front porch. Anyone walking by would think it is just another well-kept, upper-middle class home. And that's as it should be.

In fact, the lower floor houses the offices of the CIA's Berlin Station Chief, three field agents, and their one secretary. Upstairs are two large document rooms; an equipment room that includes arms, ordnance, and the chemicals and thermite grenades needed for destroying every machine and slip of paper in the building in the event of a successful Soviet invasion; a communications center manned by four teams of two specialists each, 24 hours a day, seven days a week, linked to all Berlin operatives, USAREUR Headquarters in Heidelberg, and the CIA's Washington, D.C., offices at 2430 E Street NW; and a conference room used primarily as a "war room" of sorts when the collective minds of the office are put to work on a particularly nasty problem with a detailed classified map of Berlin covering an entire wall. A full bathroom upstairs and one just off of Nick's office downstairs make late nights (routine) and overnights (rare except in the communications room) little more than a minor inconvenience. A kitchenette to the right of the downstairs foyer makes the entire affair seem like the well-ordered office of a small-town law or accounting firm with the notable exception of a roof that fairly bristles with antennae. That's it; thirteen people at the center of America's clandestine intelligence effort in Cold War Berlin working out of an ordinary house more than seventy years old. Of course, those numbers don't include a variety of freelancers, and the men and women scattered around Berlin working at the numerous American military, State Department, and private commercial sites whose efforts augment the work of the core group under Nick Temple's immediate command.

Terry, the office's lone secretary, is already seated at her desk. She came over from the OSS when the CIA was organized in '47. Nick asked her to accompany his newly-formed group to Berlin and she readily agreed. She sees Nick on the closed circuit monitor at her desk, and with the push of a button on the side of her phone buzzes the Station Chief into the building. The place is already humming with activity as Nick steps in.

Terry types the morning's Situation Report for the U.S. Mission from Arnie Miller's dictated notes. Nick grabs the comms center's overnight dispatches as Ben Sacolick, one of the office's communications specialists, is setting them in a box on the corner of Terry's desk. Nick gives them an initial cursory view. Arnie Miller breezes by on his way to a meeting at Berlin Brigade HQ. Another typewriter can be heard clacking away in one of the other first floor offices.

"Anything for the brass, Nick?" Miller asks.

"Keep it light, as usual. The less said, the better."

"SOP. Will do."

Miller leaves through the same door Nick just entered.

"Are the newspapers here?"

"They're on your desk. Coffee?"

"Sure. Thanks."

"Bob Arnold called on the secure line."

"Did he say what it was about?"

"No. But he'll be back in the office by twelve thirty our time if you want to ring him back."

"Got it. Thanks."

Terry heads for the coffee pot in the small kitchen. Nick walks into his office, hangs up his overcoat on the corner coatrack, and has a seat at his desk. As he does every morning, Nick scans the headlines of three newspapers looking for clues to what his counterparts on the other side of the Iron Curtain might be up to. This routine Wednesday morning is no different.

He first peruses *Neues Deutschland*, the official paper of the ruling Socialist Unity Party of Germany. From there he moves to *Pravda*, the organ of the Soviet Communist Party. He finishes up with a once over of *Izvestia*, the Soviet Union's official government newspaper. The word "Pravda" means truth, and the word "Isvestia" means news, which naturally leads to a typically cynical Russian joke: "There is no truth in the news, and no news in the truth."

While certain the joke accurately portrays the state of journalism in Soviet Russia, Nick's job is to see if he can wring any information from the papers that might reveal Soviet intentions, long-term or otherwise. Today's editions are of particular interest given the date: March 3, 1954, the first anniversary of the death of Josef Stalin. Throw into the mix the fact that two days earlier the U.S. announced a successful hydrogen bomb test in the South Pacific and the three papers might actually have something of use to Nick and his fellow spooks.

Terry brings in a cup of hot, black coffee.

"Thanks."

She leaves, closing the office's door behind her, and returns to typing the morning's SitRep.

Nick wades through the newspapers' various declarations of annual production in the workers' paradise exceeding the most recent five-year plan's goals by 150 percent, and stories praising the socialist heroism of this worker and that party member. He barely notes the routine condemnation of colonial imperialism in a variety of third world venues, the predictable outrage at western adventurism, and lurid, if fabricated, reports of rampant drug addiction, promiscuity, and other typically capitalist criminal activity on the streets of any city in the West. Today's capitalist cesspool of choice is Athens.

The Bikini Atoll test is the object of particularly imaginative vitriol expressed, predictably, in exactly the same language in all three papers: references to deliberately promoting "nuclear Armageddon," and "unprovoked, naked aggression" destructive to the tireless efforts of the "heroic workers of all peace-loving socialist countries" followed by nearly identical quotes from Walter Ulbricht in *Neues Deutschland*, and Nikita Krushchev in both *Pravda* and *Izvestia* about the ongoing global struggle of the proletariat and indigenous national movements to be free from the criminal threat of weapons of mass destruction being deployed by reckless capitalists and corrupt, antiquated colonial imperialists.

"Blah, blah, fucking blah," Nick says to no one in particular.

The fact that the East German and Soviet leaders would be in perfect alignment on such an important issue is no surprise. What is revealing, however, is the substance of First Secretary Krushchev's declaration on the anniversary of Stalin's death once again eulogizing the glorious leadership of the man who, more than any other man, was responsible for socialism's victory over the evil forces of fascism in the Great War for the Fatherland, the Russians' preferred moniker for World War II. Krushchev is quoted comparing that struggle to the struggle against western adventurism so clearly displayed in the irresponsible development and deployment of cataclysmic weapons around the globe.

Nick sees Krushchev's posturing for what it is: a declaration to the West that there will be no softening of the Soviet position in the Cold War in spite of the death of the ruthless murderer Stalin, and that Krushchev will follow in Stalin's hardline footsteps when it comes to the Soviet Union's geopolitical posture.

"Bring it on, fat man," Nick thinks to himself.

As he does every morning he's in his office, once he finishes with the newspapers he turns his attention to a pile of dispatches, particularly those from CIA operatives working under various titles for America's embassies in Europe.

CHAPTER 3

SOUNDING BOARD

There are a few men whose counsel Nick Temple seeks. Bob Arnold, a grizzled veteran of the country's two most recent wars, is one of those men.

Arnold's reputation is sufficient to give him unquestioned access to any piece of information the Agency collects. While others are relegated to access on a need-to-know basis, Arnold is presumed to need to know everything the Agency knows. His experience is so broad, and his mind so nimble that it would be a waste to compartmentalize his responsibilities. Fortunately, the Director of Central Intelligence worked with him personally during both wars and knew his inestimable value to America's Cold War intelligence efforts when Arnold came knocking on the Agency's door upon his retirement from the Army in June of 1953.

A tough kid from America's hardscrabble heartland, Arnold joined the Army out of desperation after graduating from high school in 1933. A promised scholarship to Purdue evaporated when a local big shot decided to throw his weight around on behalf of his underachieving son. Arnold's parents, as poor as any in America at the height of the Great Depression, had made it clear at the beginning of his senior year that come June they would no longer be able to support him. As the national unemployment rate hovered around 30 percent, Bob Arnold packed a small cardboard suitcase and bade his parents farewell. With five one dollar bills in his pocket, he hitchhiked to Gary, Indiana, in search of an Army recruiter who'd been through his hometown earlier that spring.

Twenty-one years and two wars later Arnold's reputation as perhaps the best military intelligence analyst in the country provides him with the sort of access few are granted to the stacks of information pouring in every day to the CIA's Washington, D.C., headquarters.

Nick looks at his watch: 1430 hours Berlin time; 0830 hours eastern standard time. Arnold's already been in his D.C. office for two hours.

Nick steps out of his office and heads upstairs to the comms center. Communications specialist Sacolick is on duty.

"Ben, I need to get Bob Arnold on the secure line."

"Yes, sir. Have a seat, and I'll have him up in a minute."

Ben turns to a large bank of telecommunications equipment to connect the Zehlendorf office to CIA Headquarters in D.C. As Sacolick works, Nick turns over in his mind what *Pravda* and *Izvestia* had to say about Kruschchev.

"Go ahead, sir. Line three."

Nick pushes the flashing button on the phone in front of him and picks up the receiver.

"Bob? Nick Temple here."

"Nick, good to hear from you. What can I do for you?"

The connection, as always, is perfect and encrypted. Anyone trying to listen in would hear nothing more than electronic gibberish impossible to decipher without the latest top secret piece of electronic gadgetry produced by the technical wizards at the National Security Agency.

"Returning your call. Did you see the piece in *Pravda* on Krushchev?" Nick continues.

"Yeah. Same garbage they ran in *Izvestia*."

"Exactly. What do you make of it?"

"It's tough to say. I thought Krushchev had convinced everyone about the size of his balls when he had Beria shot."

"It almost seemed like a warning to me."

"I thought so, too. But that doesn't make much sense, unless it's for internal consumption. I mean, why tell the rest of us that you're looking to stir up some shit? You lose the element of surprise."

"It's pretty damn generic, though," Nick suggests.

Bob Arnold agrees. "Good point. He sends a warning, or reassurance, to anyone doubting how tough he is, and it's so general that if he's actually got something planned, there's no way to make anything specific of it."

"Anything come across your desk that you might be able to tie it to? Troop movements? Cancelled leaves? Big shots getting shuffled around? You know, the usual."

"Not a thing. I'm up to my eyeballs in paper, but I haven't seen anything I could connect to the articles. Anything over there in Berlin?"

"Nada. Look, keep me posted if anything pops up on your radar screen."

"Always. You do the same."

"You got it."

"Ellie and the kids doing well?"

"I guess so. I hardly ever see them, although I did have the pleasure of driving a pair of distant, sullen teenagers to school this morning. Goes with the territory."

"That's a fact. Anything else I can do for you?"

"That's it, Bob. Thanks for that. Everything all right your way?"

"Oh, yeah. Same old shit. They pretend to pay me, and I pretend to work. Just like the Army."

Nick laughs.

"All right, my friend. Terry said you called."

"Just wanted to talk about our Commie friends. I think we covered it."

"Okay. We'll be in touch."

"Out here."

Nick hangs up, satisfied that he's got it right, and that's what worries him.

CHAPTER 4

POUNDING THE PAVEMENT

Two men in dark, wool overcoats, fedoras pulled low, work to stay warm on another cold night in Berlin. They stand in the shadow of a building's entryway near the intersection of Mauerstrasse and Friedrichstrasse, just north of Zimmerstrasse. The streets are nearly deserted as midnight approaches.

"Why make him go through the checkpoint?"

Arnie Miller has been complaining about the night's plan from the moment the directive arrived in the office.

"Orders from D.C.," Nick patiently responds.

He checks his watch, a 1953 Bulova Commuter. The target is 10 minutes late. Not a good sign.

"I don't like it."

"It's got to look like a routine crossing. They don't want any flak about the Americans meddling in the internal affairs of the DDR," Nick explains for about the third time.

"Christ. They're gonna get it anyway. Why not make it safe?"

"That's the way it's going down, so let's just keep on our toes."

"What the hell's taking so long?"

"You have more coffee than usual today?"

"Nah. Maybe. Yeah, but I just don't like the setup. April Fool's Day, another bad omen."

"How about if we calm down and stay focused?"

Nick has to agree with his countryman and fellow CIA agent Arnie Miller. If America's latest potential acquisition–the "target"–from the Deutsche Demokratische Republik actually makes it through the night, no one will be more surprised than Nick.

A young submarine commander during the war, the target chafes at the East German Navy's post-war role of being little more than an extension of the Army's border patrol. He wants out. Better yet, from the American point of view, his disgust with his Soviet overlords has pushed him to the point of treason. He contacted the American Mission in Berlin more than a month ago about the possibility of working for the Americans, and the Mission contacted Miller.

Miller and Temple evaluated the target and concluded that due to his egotistical and mercurial nature he would not make a stable, continuous source of reliable HUMINT, human intelligence; too many personality flaws and too much potential maintenance. However, they recommended that he be offered asylum and some cash for the purposes of gaining whatever information he currently possesses. After that, he'd be on his own. Washington agreed, and the crossover was set up for tonight.

"That should be him."

Nick sees the car, a 1952 Russian black Pobeda, at the same moment Arnie does. Stopping at the checkpoint should be routine, but something's wrong. An American M.P. steps out of the checkpoint booth and orders the driver to halt. Instead, the car slowly weaves towards the checkpoint until it slides to the right before lurching to a stop on the sidewalk. Another M.P. sprints out of the checkpoint guardhouse to inspect the car. With his M1911 .45 caliber service pistol drawn, the M.P. opens the driver's side door. A former submariner who survived five years of duty in the North Atlantic during World War II rolls out of the driver's seat and falls to the sidewalk, dead from a bullet to the back of his head.

"We're outta here."

Miller doesn't have to be told twice.

"Damn! I knew it."

"It's a long shot, but work your contacts at the 287th tomorrow. See if he or the car had any docs."

"Maybe D.C. will let us work the next one our way."

"Don't count on it."

They separate at the next corner, surrendering the field after having lost an anonymous Cold War battle, a battle that will be forgotten by history long before anyone claims the body of its lone casualty.

CHAPTER 5

HAPPY HOLIDAYS

The Athens apartment of Mika Ioannou is already suffused with the rich smell of *arnaki souvlas*, roasted lamb on a spit. Twenty-four years old, and a recent university graduate, Mika, a black-haired, green-eyed beauty, straddles the traditional world of her Greek forebears and the modern world of near continual political crisis as Greece struggles to find its post-Civil War identity. The surprising strength of the radical left in mainstream Greek politics after the collapse of the political center in 1952 has created an atmosphere of uncertainty for many, excitement for some, and danger for a few. Mika's own vision of Greece's future is simple and relatively apolitical: a modern, western state that values its glorious and distant past while building a future on the contributions of all of its citizens. For her, the future is about practicality; monarchies are pointless, the oppression of women is a waste, and wrangling over the fine points of different branches of Marxism is just plain silly. She stands ready to roll up her sleeves and put her degree in public health to work for the good of all of the people of Greece. But not today.

Today, Easter Sunday, 1954, she prepares dinner for herself and her on-again, off-again companion, Niko Lendaris, a hot-headed Leninist whose screeds she tolerates given his striking resemblance, from head to foot, to Michelangelo's David. An open bottle of Ouzo and two shot glasses on the kitchen table should get the afternoon off to a fine start.

Niko bursts into the apartment in a dark mood. His mercurial nature appears deeply rooted in Peloponnesian politics. In fact, he's a fraud who has discovered that a turbulent persona dressed in the trappings of exotic political dogma holds a strange attraction for young university co-eds willing to cozy up to a statuesque radical. But Mika is no average co-ed, and Niko is finding the results of his efforts less than satisfactory.

"You're late," Mika observes as she begins to carve the lamb on the spit. Her rich voice is full-throated; her tone is direct but not scolding.

Niko ignores her. He pours himself a shot of Ouzo, throws it back, and sits at the small linoleum table a few feet from where Mika works.

"First one today?"

"Out of this bottle," he replies as he pours another shot. Before Mika can respond, he drains the glass again.

"Slow down. We can drink and make love after dinner, unless that's too much bourgeois decadent happiness for you all in one day."

Niko explodes.

"Can we drop the fucking politics for just one day? I'm sick of hearing about the decadent this, the oppressed that, the goddamn chained fucking masses. It's all bullshit! Bullshit!"

Niko springs from his chair, knocking it over in the process, and storms straight for the apartment door he'd entered moments earlier.

Mika is unperturbed by this latest petulant outburst. She looks for a way to make it clear he is never to return. Her eyes settle on the sizable lamb still on the spit.

"Niko, darling. Don't forget your dinner."

Mika picks up the lamb and hurls what was supposed to be the prelude to an afternoon in the sack in a graceful arc towards the infuriated, pseudo-Marxist Niko. As the lamb catapults towards him something catches his ear and he turns to face her just in time to see the descending spit of lamb, sharpened-point first like an Olympic javelin, head straight for his heart. The spit impales him and would have gone far deeper but for the succulent lamb still skewered in place. It went deep enough. Niko stares for a moment in disbelief before falling backwards, dead before he hits the ground, the victim of an Easter dinner gone badly awry.

Mika's first thought is to salvage the lamb from the spit. Instead, after satisfying herself that her dinner companion is quite dead, she sits down to a meal of tzatziki, stuffed grape leaves, pita, and Ouzo as she contemplates when she should call the Athenian police, and what she should tell them when they finally arrive.

CHAPTER 6

THE HOME FRONT

Eleanor Temple sits in her home in the Lichterfelde District of Berlin longing for life back in the States. When Nick told her he was being named the Station Chief for Berlin, she was initially excited about returning to Europe. She hadn't been back since right before the War, and her memories from her year abroad while at Vassar were typically romantic: studying at the Sorbonne, skiing in Gstaad, the Festival of San Fermin in Pamplona. All of the high times were calling her back to the Continent and she insisted Nick accept the position.

Now she wishes she had shown some reticence so she could blame her husband for her endless ennui. Barred by Company rules from getting too close to the locals, subjected to carefully circumscribed travel restrictions, purposefully separated from the higher social circle of the American Military Officers' wives, living under a benevolent but watchful eye, Eleanor finds that being the wife of CIA Section Chief Nick Temple has little to offer from a social point of view. Even Nick's preference for the occasional opera at the Theater Des Westens is one she doesn't share.

She drives her two teenage children to and from the Thomas A. Roberts school for American dependents each day, does the daily grocery shopping either "on the economy" or at the American Commissary, muddles through the routine household chores, sees the sights in Berlin again, and again, and again, and visits a few of the places she spent part of her capricious youth during brief summer vacations with Nick and the children. By her seventh year in Berlin, she is more than restless, she wants out.

While her Vassar classmates were often quite naturally paired with young men from Yale, she ended up with Harvard's Nick Temple. Their hasty marriage within a week of graduating in 1939 barely disguised the early February birth of their daughter the next year. While both families publicly stuck with the myth of a premature birth, their eight pound, twelve ounce daughter made the story a difficult sell. A second child, this one a son, followed before the year was out. And while Eleanor works hard at being a model wife and mother, she can never shake the feeling that her marriage is a trap she might have escaped if she and Nick had shown more self-control.

As she sits looking out the kitchen window of a house confiscated by the United States Army in 1945 and now owned by the Department of Defense, she is certain she knows exactly what she'll be doing each day, and she wonders how much longer she'll be able to do any of it. She wonders if she'll be able to return after their pending summer vacation stateside.

The phone rings. She knows what's coming, but she picks it up anyway.

"Hello."

"Hey, Ellie. It's me."

"Don't tell me."

"It can't be helped. You and the kids go ahead and have dinner without me."

"I'll put your picture on the table so they won't forget what you look like."

"Don't be that way. It's not something I can help."

"It never is, Nick."

She hangs up and goes back to staring out the window.

On the other end, Nick stares into the receiver for a moment before hanging up. He checks his watch, grabs his jacket from the coatrack in the corner of his office, and heads out, one man working in the shadow of the Iron Curtain to keep his wife and children, and millions of other wives and children, safe.

CHAPTER 7

IT'S A LIVING

With his wife's sarcasm still ringing in his ears, Nick drives to Tempelhof Airport. A tip from a German pharmacist shortly after lunch alerted him to a shipment of black market weapons and morphine supposedly arriving tonight from Istanbul. He made the usual phone calls and now has to follow up. Normally he'd let the local gendarmes handle the matter, but the inclusion of weapons in the tip means the CIA needs to take a look.

He pulls up to a German Polizei office in the heart of the sprawling complex at Tempelhof, parks his car, and walks into the office's small reception area. He finds four undercover agents from KRIPO, Germany's Kriminalpolizei, and a handful of Air Police from the 7350th Air Base Squadron, the main USAF unit based out of Tempelhof, all sitting around as if they're waiting for a bus. Nobody stirs when Nick comes in, not even the familiar faces. Nick has seen more activity at a morgue.

"All right, I'll bite. What the hell's going on?"

Air Force Captain Dan Moorefield speaks up.

"The flight never arrived, sir."

"Were we tracking it out of Istanbul?"

"Affirmative."

Nick can't stand these guys who say things like "Affirmative." Why the hell can't he just say "yes"? He is about to make a snide remark when he checks himself knowing his irritation has much to do with his most recent conversation with his wife, and little to do with the Air Force Captain's understandable immersion in military culture.

"Did it go down?"

"That's what it looked like initially, that they were going down east of Crete. They were losing altitude, and Air Traffic Control couldn't raise them on the radio."

"What happened?"

"Just after reaching the northeast coast, slightly west of an area known as Vai, they started to climb again. It wasn't long before they were back at normal cruising altitude, heading back to Istanbul."

"What the hell was that?"

"We're not sure. We've got people in Istanbul checking it out. You might want to get your guys on it, too."

"Is there anything of note around, what did you say, Vai?"

"Right, Vai. Not much. Mostly palm trees and beaches. There's an old monastery nearby, and a small town, but that's about it."

"Anyone at the monastery, or are we talking about some 9th century ruins?"

"My understanding is that the monastery is operational, sir."

"Shit. All right. We'll have a look at it. Let me know if the Air Force comes up with anything."

"Affirmative."

"I'm out of here. I've got some repair work to do at home."

Nick turns to leave. As he opens the office door, he stops and turns to address Captain Moorefield.

"What kind of aircraft are we talking about, Captain?"

"C-47, sir. Nothing fancy."

"Does it have the range to fly non-stop from Istanbul to Berlin?"

"Absolutely, sir. With room to spare."

"Anything unusual about using a C-47 to go from Istanbul to Berlin?"

"Not a thing, sir. I'm sure the flight plan was identical to hundreds of sorties."

"Okay. Thanks, Captain. Keep me posted."

Nick closes the door behind him and hopes he can make it home before the kitchen table has been cleared of the evening's dishes and his picture.

CHAPTER 8

WATCHING THE WATCHER

No more than a week after further eroding his relationship with his wife by wasting an evening at Tempelhof, Nick works through a file sent over to CIA by Berlin Brigade. A French sergeant has been going around conning U.S. Army privates into loaning him money. A few of the more conscientious privates set aside their personal embarrassment and reported the activity to their Battalion S2, the staff intelligence and security officer. HQ is pretty sure the guy isn't anything more than a two-bit con man, but they've asked Nick to take a look at it to make sure there isn't something more there. Nick's certain HQ has it right. He starts dictating a memo suggesting that Brigade's French friends transfer the asshole to their colonial Army in Algeria to find out how the locals in North Africa react when they don't get paid back. He's interrupted by a knock on the door. Arnie Miller peaks in.

"Come on in, Arnie. What can I do for you?"

"Cliff Thompson," Arnie says as he sits in a chair in front of Nick's desk.

"What's he got?"

"Some local national has got her hooks into our friend Vasily Malenkov."

"East or west?"

"West. No doubt. He wants to see what she's up to."

"A face to face?"

"That's what he has in mind."

"Absolutely. I'd love to get inside Malenkov's operation. The guy's a complete prick. What do we know about this woman?"

"A knockout. A war widow."

"Sounds pretty typical. Starving local looks around and sees the potential for a sweet deal shacking up with the occupiers."

"I think this one's different."

"All right. Let's see what he gets. Tell him to go slowly, not that it'll do any good. He's always been his own man."

"I'll do it."

"Is that it?"

Arnie stands up to leave.

"Yeah. What are you working on?"

"Seeing if I can't get a French chiseler sent to Algiers."

Arnie laughs.

"How is it you get all the good assignments?"

"Rank has its privileges, my friend."

They both laugh.

"Hey, we ever get anything from the 287th on our dead submariner?"

"The car was clean, and so was the body."

"It was a longshot. Okay. Thanks, Arnie."

Arnie closes the office door behind him and Nick returns to his dictation.

CHAPTER 9

OUT OF THE FRYING PAN

Vanessa Porter's first steps into the gray Berlin dawn are purposeful and brisk. Her stride and the look on her face say she's in a hurry to put the night behind her. The walk of shame. Cliff Thompson has seen the stride and look before, and after two months of watching, he decides the time is right. He keeps pace on the other side of Kaiserdamm. She stops at a corner to let some early traffic pass. Thompson seizes the opportunity to cross over and walk behind her. She sees him cross in her peripheral vision before she resumes walking. She noticed him when she first came out of Malenkov's apartment building. He's the same man she's seen at least half a dozen times in the last month. She's as curious as she is frightened. She knows an illicit affair with the local KGB Operations Chief has its risks. Could the man no more than ten steps behind her be one of those risks?

She ducks into the Bismarck Café. Thompson follows and calmly sits at her small table just inside the street-facing window.

"Doesn't Vasily cook breakfast for you?"

"I'm certain I don't know what you're talking about."

"Can the act, sister. You know exactly what I'm talking about."

"Why should my eating habits be any concern of yours, whoever you are?"

"They aren't. But Vasily Malenkov's are."

A waiter approaches. Thompson takes over.

"Zwei Tassen Kaffee und ein Kännchen Schokolade, bitte."

"Etwas zu essen?"

"Nein, danke."

The waiter looks at Vanessa. She looks away.

"Bitte."

The waiter departs, and Vanessa looks back at Thompson.

"Maybe I'd like something more than coffee and hot chocolate."

"What do you cook for Vasily?"

"Don't be ridiculous. I haven't cooked for anyone since the war."

"Your husband?"

"If you're going to insist on being a boor, I'd at least like to know your name."

"We'll get to that. You had to know this was coming. I haven't been discreet."

Vanessa pauses. He's right. With the stakes in the Cold War getting higher every day, she knew that her fling with Malenkov would get the attention of the West. Whether it was the Americans, the Brits, or her own West German government she couldn't say. But she knew full well that once she went down this road eventually she'd have company. And that was the plan.

The waiter brings two cups of coffee and a small pitcher of hot chocolate.

"Danke."

"Bitte."

Vanessa waits for the waiter to leave before speaking up.

"What took you so long?"

"I had to make sure he was interested."

"You've gone from being a boor to insulting me. Congratulations."

Cliff Thompson has to admit that any sane man with a heartbeat would be interested in Vanessa Porter. Distant glimpses of her over two months pale in comparison with the effect of being face-to-face and less than three feet away from her. He's certain her 5 feet 10 inch frame with legs that go on forever made her young husband the envy of his Wehrmacht peers right up until his execution for being implicated in a plot to assassinate the Führer. Being a war widow gives her deep Nordic beauty a tragic air that makes her nearly irresistible. Clearly, he thinks to himself, Vasily Malenkov agrees.

He throws a fifty-mark note on the table and stands up.

"It's probably less than you got for last night, but it'll cover breakfast. I'll be in touch."

He turns and leaves, quickly mingling with the growing crowd of Berliners making their way to work.

Vanessa stares at the fifty-mark note and hesitates for a moment before folding it and placing it in her pocket. She pours a small bit of hot chocolate into her coffee and stirs it idly wondering if she hasn't made a fatal mistake.

"The Americans it is," she thinks to herself. She feels a slight shiver go up her spine. The thrill she sought, the thrill of being part of something dangerous, is returning.

CHAPTER 10

THE FOX AND THE HENHOUSE

Vasily Malenkov sits in his office at the Soviet Trade Mission building, a thin disguise for a KGB satellite, contemplating the evening he is about to spend with Vanessa Porter. He knows she's got him on a short leash. That much is clear. What he is having trouble understanding is why he cares. His current affair with "the Porter woman" as he likes to think of her, while certainly an attractive diversion, has become uncharacteristically complex. She wants to end the entire matter, a sensible position given that the physical aspects of their relationship have recently been overshadowed by the unexpected appearance of some tiresome emotions. And while she is almost painfully beautiful, the fact that she is in her late 30s is again uncharacteristic of his previous affairs. It's almost as if she considers herself his peer, something he is quite unaccustomed to.

He has found over the years that women, girls really, in their late teens or early twenties who are tired of the depravations of post-war Berlin are the most pleasant and pliant companions. Simple trinkets he acquires through the coercive power of his office delight such women who are then eager to show their gratitude. The Porter woman is not so easily impressed and the effort to maintain his relationship with her has gotten all out of proportion to what he is gaining from it. He blames the Americans and their self-righteous Marshall Plan for elevating the average Berliner's standard of living, particularly of those living in the western zones, and he chafes at the possibility that he may have to look to the wretched East for future conquests.

He is resolute as he gets up to leave the Albrechtstrasse building. He will end the affair with Vanessa Porter after their dinner tonight. Before leaving his office he goes to the wall-length credenza behind his desk, pours himself a shot of vodka, raises his glass, mutters "Pod Stolom!" to himself, and throws back the shot. Thus fortified, he marches out of his office towards his rendezvous.

CHAPTER 11

RED SQUARE ONE

As the Cold War gets into full swing in the first half of the 1950s, the tension between East and West is global in scale and cataclysmic in consequence. Vast areas of Africa and Asia present new challenges to American policymakers intent on implementing the country's still-evolving containment policy. The recently formed National Security Council's virtual call to arms in NSC-68 envisions the United States as the only credible bulwark against world-wide Communist aggression. The fear of collusion between Soviet Russia and Mao's Red China drives policy decisions at nearly every level of government. The development of the unthinkably destructive hydrogen bomb means that the specter of the literal end of the world now hangs over the increasingly tense relationship, if it can be called that, between the world's two Superpowers.

As global as the struggle between the two nations is, there is no spot on the globe where they are face to face on a daily basis like they are in the single most active espionage and counterespionage venue of the Cold War: Berlin. What might happen next in Berlin is anyone's guess. Nick Temple isn't just anyone, and he isn't paid to guess.

Tonight he nurses a German pilsner as he waits in a small restaurant in Berlin's Steglitz district in the American Sector. In the year plus since Stalin's death, Berlin has been one of the few conduits of reliable information for the West about the ensuing power struggle in the Kremlin. The December 1953 murder of Stalin's trusted and ruthless

KGB chief, Lev Beria, came as a shock to counterintelligence types all across Europe. It's up to men like Nick Temple to figure out what's coming next.

Nick has been through tougher scrapes, World War II to name one. But he's always been able to read the tea leaves, to figure out who is up and who is down. As long as Stalin was alive a certain insane predictability characterized the moves of Nick's counterparts on the other side of the Iron Curtain. Nick's fluency in German and Russian, and his uncanny ability to accurately predict major Soviet moves during World War II made him an obvious choice for Berlin Station Chief when the CIA was organized under the National Security Act of 1947.

The early years were lean, but budgets for clandestine operations have ballooned since the truce was signed at Panmunjom, and now the Berlin group finds itself awash in cash. Nick uses it wisely, developing assets like Cliff Thompson, a Signal Corps and OSS vet who came back to Berlin after a brief stint in Trieste at the end of the war.

Thompson is late again. He's a freelancer. That makes him harder to control, harder to pin down. Being late is getting to be a habit for him, a bad habit. But he delivers. His intel is always rock solid, and Nick's not about to chew him out like some bully schoolmaster for being tardy every now and then.

But waiting is dangerous. Too much time in one spot goes against all the rules, especially at night. Just as Nick decides to leave, Thompson walks in. Third booth on the left, under the Berliner Kindl Bier sign. Nick, against his better judgment, decides to stay.

Thompson motions to the waiter to bring a beer as he slides into the booth. He pulls an envelope out of his jacket pocket and pushes it across the table to Nick.

"You owe me big time on this one."

"Getting too hot for you?"

"Never."

"What, then?"

"Your masters are going to shit when they see it."

The waiter delivers the beer. Nick hands him 10 Deutschmarks, and the waiter digs the change out of his apron pocket. Thompson hits the beer hard. Nick stares at Thompson as the waiter counts out the change. Nick is looking for any sign that Thompson has lost his edge. It's part of the job, just routine observation that Nick undertakes whenever he interfaces with an asset. The waiter leaves. Nick puts some of the change in his pocket, leaving a decent tip–trinkgeld–for the waiter. He then pulls out a business envelope, places it on the table, and pushes it over to Thompson who quickly stuffs it into the breast pocket of his overcoat.

"There's a bonus in there."

"And I didn't get you anything."

"I prefer it that way. And don't bother with a thank you note."

Thompson takes another long draw on the beer.

"Krushchev is starting to muscle up."

"More executions?"

"Much bigger."

"An all-out pogrom?"

"My source says he's making a move against the West."

"Why?"

"To make sure everyone in Russia thinks he's about the meanest son of a bitch on the planet."

"What about the Beria hit? Didn't that do it for him?"

"Old news."

"He's got to be getting heat from somewhere. What kind of move?"

"It's not clear. But he's focused on the Navy."

Nick's mind flashes to the murdered East German Navy officer who was about to defect.

"Shit. That means it could come anywhere."

"We've got time. No one thinks they're ready. Maybe next year."

"What about Tehran?"

"Bringing back Mossadegh?"

"Why not?"

"Not going to happen. I'm sure of it. The last thing the Soviets need is to tangle with that crowd."

"That's too thin. I can't sell it. You know these guys. They want action now, not a year from now, and they always smell a plant."

"It is what it is. The rest is up to you and your friends."

As Thompson drains his beer, Nick reminds him, "They're your friends, too."

"Right. Thanks for the beer. Sorry I was late. Believe me. It was worth it."

"Hookers in Kreuzberg?"

"I'm getting too predictable."

Without waiting for a reply, Thompson slides out of the booth and heads for the door. Nick puts Thompson's envelope in his pocket, lights a cigarette, and thinks about what will be left of the world if the Soviet Navy attacks the West a year from now.

CHAPTER 12

CLOUDS IN THE CRYSTAL BALL

Nick Temple sits in his Berlin office. As is so often the case, he has his nose buried in a file's operational report. This report is from Cliff Thompson, the one delivered in the Steglitz Bierstube. It summarizes the results of three months of surveillance of one German national named Vanessa Porter.

"Thompson is right," Nick thinks to himself. "This is dynamite."

After a brief scan of the TOP SECRET report, Nick goes back through it, bit by bit.

TO: NTemple/SCBerlin

FROM: CThompson/SOB

SUBJECT: Vanessa Porter

DATES: 1 March 1954 – 30 May 1954

RATIONALE: Subject's Relationship with Vasily Ivanovitch Malenkov, KGB Operations Chief, Berlin Sector

FIRST CONTACT: 3 May 1954

MOST RECENT CONTACT: 29 May 1954

Thompson's report, besides the not-so-subtle reference to himself as a son of a bitch, is all business. He notes the subject's history as the widow of a Wehrmacht officer executed for his participation in a conspiracy to assassinate the Führer in 1940. Four years before Operation Valkyrie! Somehow she survived the war in spite of being surrounded by her own hostile government until she was surrounded by the hostile governments of strangers. Nick is impressed with the widow and her late husband. He flips to six photographs of Vanessa Porter taken by Thompson included at the end of the report. No doubt about it; she's an impressive woman on a number of levels.

The narrative that follows notes the May 1st contact at the Bismarck Café with three more in May. Nick's brow furrows. Four contacts in a single month is pushing it. This Vanessa Porter is already at risk. Malenkov's reputation as a stone cold killer is well-deserved and well-documented. He gets results, which explains Moscow's indifference to his decidedly western tastes in women and other black market luxuries ordinary Russians can only dream about.

Each of Thompson's three contacts with Porter after the Bismarck Café gets its own write up. Thompson is a freelancer, but he's thorough and reasonably careful. He never tells Porter where or when they'll meet ahead of time. Instead, through surveillance he determines likely locations during different times of day and turns them into spontaneous meetings once he confirms she and he aren't being tailed. Nick is once again impressed.

His report of their first meeting after the Bismarck Café details her desire to get out of the relationship with Malenkov. Thompson notes he instructed her on how to leverage the possibility of a breakup; just the prospect might get Malenkov off his game, and mistakes are usually profitable. After much discussion, she acquiesces. "Cold-hearted bastard," Nick reflects. "Perfect for this line of work."

At their next meeting, Porter reports to Thompson that Malenkov is drinking more, a likelihood Thompson predicted. Malenkov spends most of his time with Porter bragging about contacts back in Moscow and what kind of life he might be able to provide for her given his connections as a well-placed member of the Communist Party. Porter sees the conversation as a threat rather than a proposal. Thompson agrees, but convinces her to return to Malenkov at least one more time. The report notes his off-color, sexual suggestions on how Porter can get more out of him. Nick cringes slightly, wondering if Porter took Thompson's advice.

The final meeting between Thompson and Porter is a goldmine. Porter puts the squeeze on the breakup, and Malenkov just keeps drinking. At one point, he threatens her should she decide to leave him. When she accuses him of acting beneath himself by threatening a woman, he is initially reduced to tears. "This guy's a real asshole," Nick thinks to himself. After another two shots of vodka, Malenkov dries the tears, puffs up, and begins to slur his way through another round of what a big shot he is, both in the KGB and the Communist Party. It seems he just can't help himself, and that's when he lets slip his inside track on Krushchev's strategic vision which includes a strike against the West. Malenkov follows up the slip with some sloppy bragging about the Soviet Navy, and how the West is going to find out that Krushchev is tougher than Stalin. At that moment, she wants to flee but, as Thompson instructed her, she remains. Fleeing would have tipped Malenkov off, and Thompson's report would be providing details about her pending funeral. Instead, Malenkov passes out shortly after spilling his guts. When he wakes up, Porter is still in his apartment as if nothing of consequence has happened. "Perfect," Nick thinks. She is, however, terrified all through breakfast as Malenkov probes to get some idea of what he might have said the night before. She handles the inquisition with amazing professionalism, and by the time she leaves she is certain he suspects nothing. Thompson concurs, noting, again, that the Porter woman would likely be dead if Malenkov had any suspicion about the magnitude of his screw up.

After the narrative, Thompson provides Vanessa Porter's contact information and a brief conclusion. In his estimation the HUMINT, while not specifically actionable due to its ambiguous nature, is solid and should be a catalyst for additional Agency activity aimed at verifying the intel's bona fides and fleshing out its details. He adds almost as an afterthought that Porter's life is likely in danger.

Nick takes a deep breath, exhales, and leans back in his chair for a moment to let it all sink in. He carefully reviews the report again to make sure he has the timeline of the meetings and the timing of Krushschev's potential move straight. He needs to clean up the report a bit, put more caveats and conditional language in it, and emphasize the very real possibility that Malenkov made the whole thing up just to impress Porter. That being said, the intel has to get back to Washington as soon as possible for further analysis in light of what might be coming in from other stations. Bob Arnold, his old friend at the Company with unfettered access to all Agency work product, is the perfect man for the job. Nick also resolves to sit down with Vanessa Porter, face-to-face, to see if he can figure out what drives this remarkable woman.

CHAPTER 13

PUZZLES NEED PIECES

As with any puzzle, figuring out how the first pieces fit together is the greatest challenge. The intelligence game is all about the puzzle. What looks like random chatter, a chance slip of paper, a harmless encounter or meeting, could just as easily be the key to something much larger. Even the trained eye can look right past a flicker of meaning that points in the direction of the next piece, which helps explain the piece after that, or gives deeper meaning to something or things earlier dismissed as routine. The analyst's job is to keep it all in his head so that when he stumbles onto the key, those pieces floating around in his memory stand out in a new way, with new import. It takes a special mind to excel in the analyst's world of literally thousands of bits of seemingly unrelated information, the sort of mind that belongs to Bob Arnold.

Today, as he goes through the daily briefings from a dozen different CIA stations around the world, and just as many embassies, a report from Athens catches his eye. An accidental homicide investigation uncovered some documents from the apartment of the deceased, an alleged Marxist philanderer of little note. The Athenian police thought enough of the find to pass the documents along to the American Embassy. The report in the diplomatic pouch is typically dated. More than eight weeks have passed since the incident. But the packet is at least thorough; it includes the documents: used tickets for two recent trips by the deceased to Crete, each with a handwritten list, in Russian, of what look like codenames. At the bottom of one list is the notation "Agios

Nikolaos." At the bottom of the other appears "Heraklion." The names of both cities are written in phonetic Cyrillic.

When Arnold sees the documents and report, he immediately thinks of a report his friend Nick Temple sent a few days ago that carefully, almost cryptically, hints at a Soviet naval strike against the West within a year. Is the Eastern Mediterranean the target? He brings his focus back to the report from Athens.

Arnold is impressed by the Athenian police officer who was alert enough to bring the documents to the attention of the Americans. The long-suspected direct connection between Moscow and Greek Communists might finally have some concrete proof other than just the lurid imagination of American politicians willing to see the Russians behind any challenge uttered anywhere in the world to the righteousness of absolute American supremacy. He resolves to find out what he can about the travel habits of the late Niko Lendaris, and he starts to ponder who should go to Athens to interview the woman noted in the report as Lendaris' killer, Mika Ioannou.

CHAPTER 14

GETTING A MEET AND GREET

Cliff Thompson zealously guards his independence from the routines of bureaucracy. He is almost pathologically averse to anything having the slightest appearance of government formality. Nick is certain that if he ever told Thompson he'd have to drop by the office to get paid that Thompson would tell him to shove it and he'd never hear from him again. Nick's guess is that Thompson had more than his share of bureaucracy during his time in the military and his stint in the OSS. It took Nick the better part of a year to convince Thompson to provide coherent reports that weren't simply meandering narratives. The results have been outstanding as Thompson has one of the clearest minds Nick has ever encountered in a freelancer.

Thompson is a strange contradiction. His time in the military was so distasteful – for reasons he won't discuss – that he likes to shove it to the U.S. Government any time he can. For instance, he does whatever he can to avoid paying taxes; Nick has to pay him in cash that is entered simply as a "development" expense on the debit side of the office's ledger. Thompson is constantly changing his address to thwart attempts to track him down to get him to pay alimony to his less-than-deserving wife. (Somehow, in spite of being pregnant and giving birth to a child towards the tail end of her husband's 24-month continuous absence during World War II, she and her lawyer were able to convince a judge to stick it to Cliff Thompson.) He ignores court orders, subpoenas,

IRS threats, and any static from a government that seems less than grateful for his years of sacrifice and service.

However, he's convinced that the Soviets are a bigger menace than his own government. He doesn't worry so much about the possibility of World War III, or the collapse of representative democracy at the hands of crazed communists. His worry is simple: if the Soviets ever control the country he lives in, he has no doubt that their government will be a much bigger pain in the ass than the American government is. So he's got a dog in the hunt, as he likes to say, and he spends way too many of his waking hours figuring out how to personally torment anyone who has any connection to Moscow's rulers. Much to his delight, if Thompson could ever be said to experience such an emotion, Berlin is the perfect place for him; so long as he stays within the city's limits he can thumb his nose at America's stateside authorities, and continue his life's work of "fucking with Ivan" as he likes to say. All of which makes Cliff Thompson a pain in Nick Temple's ass.

Nick would have him jailed in a New York minute if it weren't for the constant flow of actionable intel that Thompson has produced year after year. Cliff Thompson, unattached and unrepentant, has produced some of the most important pieces of intel to cross Nick's desk since his return to Berlin in 1947. Thompson's report on Vasily Malenkov and Vanessa Porter is no exception. Now it's time for Nick to take over and figure out how to use it.

Nick knows the ridiculous routine if he wants to initiate contact with Thompson. There's a window of no more than five minutes each Monday evening starting at 5 p.m. when Thompson places himself near a phone booth at one of Berlin's many U-bahn stations. The commuter crowd is his cover. This Monday Thompson stations himself near a phone at the Nürnberger Platz station. Nick retrieves the number from an encrypted list provided by Thompson at the beginning of the month, and dials.

"Thompson."

"Cliff. It's Nick. Let's talk."

"I'm listening."

"Face to face."

"No can do, Nicky. Not this week."

"What about setting up a meeting between Mrs. Porter and me?"

"Where?"

"The Wannsee Chateau."

"I'll get back to you."

Thompson hangs up, leaving Nick to think what he normally thinks after any contact with Thompson.

"What a fucking nut job."

While Nick thinks about using Porter's contact information to call her directly if Thompson doesn't call back, his phone rings. Less than a minute has passed.

"Mr. Thompson on line one."

"Thanks, Terry."

Nick pushes the flashing line one button on his phone.

"Forget your hat?"

"What?"

"Never mind. What can I do for you Cliff?"

"She'll be there. Time and day?"

"Ten in the morning. Friday."

"Have a car waiting at your office at nine."

"Afraid I'll cut out the middle man?"

"Something like that."

"All right. I'll have a car here."

Thompson hangs up leaving Nick to ponder just what the hell he has in mind.

"Ivan's not the only one he fucks with," Nick mutters.

CHAPTER 15

IT FEELS LIKE THE FIRST TIME

Nick often uses a medium-sized room on the top floor of the chateau at the U.S. Army's Wannsee Yacht Club Am Sandwerder as a secure meeting place. The installation is well-guarded, access is nicely restricted, and, the view west across the Wannsee is spectacular, particularly on this warm, early summer day.

Vanessa Porter is waiting, having been brought to the Chateau in an unmarked car driven by a German national who Nick hires from time to time. He is one of a pool of locals Nick relies on for fairly routine jobs that need to be done with discretion. Nick had him park in front of the Zehlendorf office at 9 a.m. as instructed. One minute later, Cliff Thompson got into the back seat and off they went.

The M.P. guarding the entrance to the Chateau waves Nick through as he pulls into the circular drive at the main building's entrance. The driver and car that brought Vanessa sit just past the building's entrance in the shade of one of the property's many white poplar trees.

After parking, Nick gets out with the file containing Thompson's report under his arm, enters the building, and goes immediately to the top floor. Three flights of stairs lead him to a landing. Although there are only two floors of rooms in the Chateau the ceilings of the first floor are nearly 15 feet high reflecting an aesthetic from a bygone era. Nick strides down the hall to the last room on the right, and enters.

The room is deliberately casual and contemporary. When Nick first came to Berlin, the room had all the charm of an interrogation chamber. With plenty of other facilities scattered around Berlin for the Americans to conduct interrogations, Nick decided this room should look more like a family sitting room to put those using it at ease. He asked Ellie to decorate it, and, given the typically tight budget he gave her, she did an admirable job.

Vanessa Porter sits on the room's low-slung couch along its north wall, beneath a large watercolor of sailboats heading downwind with their brightly-colored spinnakers flying. To her right is an open window whose white, gauze curtains puff and flow pushed by a faint summer breeze off the lake to the west. The room's pastel yellow walls and white trim mix with the sunshine and fresh breeze to give the room the feel of a lakeside resort.

Vanessa Porter wears a summer floral print dress with cap sleeves; her white gloves and small white purse sit beside her on the couch. She stands as Nick enters. In her heels, she is as tall as he is. They shake hands formally, one quick up and down motion as is the German custom.

"Mrs. Porter. Nick Temple. I'm so glad you could make it. Please, have a seat. Is there anything I can get you? Water? Perhaps a cup of tea?"

Vanessa sits back down as she declines his offer.

"I am delighted to meet you, Mr. Temple. And no, thank you, I had a late breakfast."

Nick sits in an upholstered leather chair opposite the couch, and sets his file down on the cherry wood coffee table between them. He knows the file's bright red stencil declaring its contents to be TOP

SECRET runs counter to the informality of the setting. He uses its stark, almost threatening presence as a reminder both to himself and the subject of the interview of the seriousness of their encounter.

"And I'm delighted to finally meet you. Cliff Thompson has told me much about you."

"I assumed Mr. Thompson had a boss, but, honestly, you're not what I pictured."

Nick laughs.

"What did you expect?"

"Perhaps a man in uniform, with lots of brass on his shoulders, stout, gruff, chewing on half of an unlit cigar."

Vanessa smiles slyly at the stereotype as Nick laughs again.

"I hope you're not disappointed."

"Not at all. Now, Mr. Temple, how may I be of assistance?"

She's all business, a trait Nick appreciates. He picks up the file and opens it.

"It will come as no surprise to you that your final meeting with Vasily Malenkov is of the most interest to me."

"When he cried like a woman?"

Nick was pretty sure that Vanessa Porter was not the sort of woman who would tolerate tears from a man. Her harsh assessment of Malenkov's weak behavior confirms his surmise. Once again, he is impressed.

"Well, honestly, yes. But I'm more interested in the substance of his claim to having privileged access to some remarkable pieces of information."

"He was boasting to cover his awful behavior of just moments earlier."

"That's how it strikes me. But can you remember anything he said while he was sober that might corroborate his drunken boast?"

"During our affair he quickly got into the habit of telling me what an important man he is back in Moscow."

"Was there a time when he seemed to be boasting more than usual?"

"The night before my first encounter with your rather crude associate, Mr. Thompson."

Nick ignores the accurate dig.

"May 3rd?"

"I believe so."

"Our log indicates he went to Moscow for the May Day celebrations. Is that consistent with what he told you?"

"That's what he said, yes. At times when he brought it up, and by it I mean his presumed exalted status, a look would come over his face, a sort of grin that said, 'I am the master, and you, you are nothing.' I am, unfortunately, too familiar with that look from men. I don't know if that makes sense to you, but that's the way it felt, particularly after he returned from Moscow."

"It does make sense. It sounds as if he wanted to tell you something that he thought would impress you, but he felt circumscribed by his duty."

"It may have been that, or it may have simply been a reaction to my attempts to break off the affair, because the same look, the same attitude came up during our next few meetings, until our last one when he was really too drunk for most of it to control his emotions, let alone his facial expressions."

"And that was the last time you saw him?"

"Yes. The next morning, actually. He's kept his distance since then. I imagine he's embarrassed by his dreadful behavior, and my presence would only serve to remind him of it. That's all worked to my advantage, quite as Mr. Thompson said it would. I must say, your associate is a boor, but he seems to know more than his share about human emotions."

Nick again ignores the invitation to take a pot shot at Thompson.

"How did you come to meet Malenkov in the first place?"

"I sought him out. He has a reputation in certain circles for a preference for women from the West. Usually younger women, though."

"And why did you seek him out?"

"It's simple, really. I sought him out with an eye towards a meeting like this. I come from a background that emphasizes service to one's people. We all have our special talents, and I am painfully aware of mine. I've been mostly idle since the end of the war, and I decided I've had enough of that."

"All business, and blunt at that," Nick thinks to himself.

"Mrs. Porter, you have been most helpful. Now, is there anything I can do for you?"

"I would demand that you take me to dinner followed by a night at the opera, but I see you're wearing a wedding band."

"Perhaps it's best to keep our relationship professional," Nick lies as he gets up from his chair.

"Perhaps not," Vanessa thinks to herself as she stands to leave. She extends her hand. They shake hands formally again.

"You have my number should you need anything else, Mr. Temple."

"I do. And please, call me Nick. I'll see you to your car."

As the car bearing Vanessa Porter in the back seat pulls away from the Wannsee Chateau, Nick can't help thinking how thoroughly enjoyable dinner and a night at the opera with such a remarkable woman would be. Discretion being the better part of valor, he resolves to leave that last rumination out of his next report to Bob Arnold.

CHAPTER 16

SOUND ADVICE

Vasily Malenkov looks forward to his meeting on the first of each month with Colonel Yevgeny Roznechenko–the KGB chief political officer for its Western Section–with an almost perverse pleasure. Malenkov is convinced that Roznechenko is nothing more than a crude apparatchik, skillful enough when it comes to ordering the execution or imprisonment of entire villages, but hopelessly outwitted in the subtler game of espionage. Malenkov views the meetings as contests that he believes he invariably wins.

As always, as soon as Malenkov enters the ponderously spacious office of Comrade Roznechenko, he greets his superior politely.

"Good morning, Comrade Colonel."

"Good morning, Vasily Ivanovitch. Please sit down."

Roznechenko would be glad to forego the meetings. They are meaningless to him. He finds out all he needs to know about Malenkov from a variety of sources. Malenkov's superior attitude is tiresome. Roznechenko tolerates it. "If Malenkov thinks I'm an idiot, he's likely to do something he'll regret someday," he has often thought to himself. And when that day comes, Roznechenko will be waiting to crush the arrogant insect. In the meantime, so long as Malenkov continues to produce useful intelligence about the West and traitors within their own ranks, Roznechenko plays along with the charade of being a slow-witted party hack from the hinterland.

Malenkov sits in one of the two leather chairs in front of the Colonel's desk.

"And how have you been, Comrade Colonel?"

"Worse than yesterday, but better than tomorrow, I'm afraid. And you?"

"A victim of my own extravagant tastes, as I'm sure you know."

"The Porter woman?"

"You are thorough as always."

"My only concern is for the well-being of the people of the Soviet Union. And there is little I won't do to protect their interests."

"The 100,000 or so who have died in the gulag thanks to your concern might not share your view," Malenkov thinks to himself.

"I've ended the matter. I must admit, I'll miss her physical gifts. But that is no matter. There is always the next one."

Roznechenko leans forward.

"I trust there is no need for additional action?"

"None, Comrade Colonel. The entire affair was grounded exclusively in physical attraction. I doubt we exchanged more than a few sentences each time we came together, in a manner of speaking."

Malenkov knows that his ability to spin such self-serving falsehoods will soon be circumscribed by the listening devices being installed in his Berlin flat. For the time being, however, he can lie with impunity, and he convinces himself he can rely on Vanessa's discretion at least on the east side of the Iron Curtain

"Excellent. Now let us review the month's operational reports."

Malenkov nods as Roznechenko opens a well-worn file on his desk. The meeting takes its customary bureaucratic turn, and Malenkov is convinced his unremarkable dalliance with Vanessa Porter, exactly like his numerous previous affairs, is of no further interest to his superiors.

CHAPTER 17

THE OTHER COLD WAR

Nick and Ellie sit side by side on the Pan Am flight from Berlin to London while their children sit across the aisle. Once in London they'll catch a BOAC Boeing 377 Stratocruiser for the transatlantic flight to New York. From there Nick will head to Grand Central Station for a train to Washington; Ellie and the kids will take a short hop to Boston where her father will pick them up for some summer vacation time on Cape Cod.

If the Berlin to London flight is any indication, putting the "family" in this summer's family vacation is going to be a challenge. Nick spent most of their time at Tempelhof on the phone, first with his secretary and then with Arnie Miller. Ellie refused to say a word to him when Nick finally joined them in the boarding area, and the flight is more of the same. Ellie speaks up when Nick pulls out a company file – an unmarked folder so as not to attract attention.

"You promised you were going to leave work behind this time."

Nick heeds the clear admonition and, without responding, simply puts the folder back in his flight bag.

"You couldn't even be bothered to sit with us in the boarding area. Honestly, Nick, I feel like a widow sometimes."

"You're right. I should have taken care of everything before I left the office this morning, but it didn't work out that way. You know it's not that kind of job, Ellie. I'm not sure what to say here."

He gets a sidelong glance from his son and daughter on the other side of the aisle. Unfortunately, their children are getting accustomed to the idea that the only time their parents seem to be willing to talk to each other is when they're arguing. Add to that the fact that Nick is rarely at home and the effect on his relationship with his children is fairly predictable. In short, he doesn't actually have a relationship with them. Years of coming home in the dead of night long after the dishes and homework have been done and the kids are in bed, excusing himself on birthdays and holidays, missing school plays and athletic events, sending Ellie as the family's lone adult representative at piano recitals, and being more at ease in the company of strangers in dark alleys than he is in the company of the parents of his children's friends have taken their toll.

His dedication to his job, to his country's security has always come first as it does with so many of the people he works with. He used to tell himself that December 7, 1941 was responsible for his singular dedication. But he knows plenty of guys who enlisted, as he had, on December 8th who went on to lead normal family lives after the war, so he stopped blaming the Japanese for his own shortcomings as a husband and father. The Temple family limps along, and Nick knows in his heart both that it's his fault and that it's not going to change.

Ellie goes back to reading *Life Magazine* while Nick gazes out the window as the DC-6 begins its final approach into Heathrow.

CHAPTER 18

ERASABLE INK

Vasily Malenkov, impeccably dressed as always in a three-piece suit, spots him as soon as he comes out of his apartment. He's seen the same man at least once before, towards the end of May. On this summer evening the man—little more than a severely thin, agitated, wide-eyed, specter—follows Malenkov who is headed to dinner by himself at his favorite Italian restaurant in all of Berlin. Malenkov has been thinking about the restaurant's specialty—garlic tomato soup—since right after lunch, and the fact that he'll have to attend to some other bit of business before enjoying his dinner annoys him.

Malenkov's flat is in Charlottenburg, in the British sector. That fact is a source of some irritation to his superiors. Malenkov finds its location close to the restaurants and shops of Bismarckstrasse and Kaiserdamm to be most satisfactory. He also finds living near the Spree River to be helpful whenever he needs to dispose of evidence of his most egregious indiscretions. However, he has resolved to acquiesce quickly should he ever be ordered to move to less opulent lodgings in the wretched Soviet Sector.

Business before pleasure, and instead of heading for the restaurant on Bismarckstrasse, Malenkov turns north for the Spree, and walks two blocks before he stops and calmly lights a cigarette. The man who has been following walks up to him, stands next to him, and lights a cigarette too, although his trembling hands make the task difficult.

"A nice evening for a walk."

"English?" Malenkov asks.

"I went to school in London, but I was born here in Berlin."

"What can I do for you?"

"Perhaps we can help each other."

"I doubt that. Get to the point, will you please? I have dinner plans."

"I know about Vanessa Porter," he whispers before taking a deep drag on his cigarette.

"So do I. If you have nothing else to offer, I'll be on my way."

"She's moved on."

"Quit being cryptic. I haven't the time."

The nervous man looks around quickly before continuing.

"An American. The CIA Station Chief."

"Walk with me, will you?"

Malenkov continues north towards the river.

"Don't you want to know what they talk about?"

"Of course I do."

"It'll cost you. Dollars or west marks, but not rubles."

"How much?"

"Five hundred American."

"You're cheap."

"Five hundred a month. I can be of great and continuous assistance."

They reach the river.

"All right. Let's walk down to the river, shall we?"

Malenkov and his rail-thin companion walk down a set of stone steps that lead about 10 feet down from the street level to a small, floating dock secured to a pair of pilings along the Spree River near the recently restored Schloss Charlottenburg. Malenkov takes a quick look around, pulls his Makarov PM from its shoulder holster under his suit jacket, and puts a 9 mm round in the stranger's gaunt throat, just above his bulging Adam's apple. The stranger at first attempts to reach for a pistol in his pocket, but the pain is too much to bear. His eyes now open wide with terror, he grabs his gushing throat with both hands and staggers backwards. He spits blood and gurgles desperately for air as Malenkov shoves him almost gently into the river. A quick look around confirms no one is in sight as the dead man, his lungs filling quickly from two separate holes, sinks below the dark river's surface.

Malenkov holsters his pistol, straightens his necktie, checks his clothes for spots of blood, climbs the stone steps back to street level, and heads for dinner.

"I suppose I could have simply told him that I don't care what they talk about," he mutters to himself as his thoughts return to the garlic tomato soup dinner waiting for him.

CHAPTER 19

A STATESIDE REUNION

Nick Temple walks down the busy third-floor hallway of the CIA's Washington, D.C., headquarters, stops, knocks on Bob Arnold's door, and opens it without waiting for an answer. Arnold, whose office is a cluttered mess as usual, looks up from his desk. An instant smile covers his face as he stands up, takes his signature half-smoked cigar out of his mouth, and greets his long-time friend.

"Nick. Come on in."

Arnold, wearing the Agency standard summer uniform of a white, short-sleeve shirt and thin black tie, comes out from behind his desk and the two old friends shake hands.

"When did you get in?"

"A couple of days ago."

"You should have let me know you were coming."

"I've got Ellie and the kids. Sort of a summer vacation. Ellie's had about all of Berlin's dreary weather and equally dreary social life she can take. She needed a break."

"Is she with you?"

"No. She took the kids up to her folks' place on Cape Cod. They're spending a week without the old man hanging around. I thought I'd come by to get some work done."

"That's fine, but when she gets back in town I'd love to see her and the kids."

"We'll set it up. What are you working on?"

Arnold sits back behind his desk, and Nick sits down in the one of two chairs in front of Arnold's desk without rolled maps, files, and other assorted junk all over it.

"Funny you should ask. I've got two things that I have a feeling might be related. Maybe you can help."

"Fire away."

"I've seen your reports on the Porter woman and her affair with Vasily Malenkov. Great stuff, but there might be less there than meets the eye."

"Agreed. I sat down with her. Maybe just some drunken, empty boasting on Malenkov's part. It's all in the reports. She's a remarkable woman. If this doesn't pan out, maybe she can help us out some other way."

"I know this Malenkov character. He's an absolute egomaniac. Like you say, there's every chance he was just trying to impress his latest girlfriend."

"Again, agreed."

"I like the Porter woman, though. My hunch is she's on the up and up. Helluva story about her husband during the war. I'm surprised they didn't hang her too."

"Cliff Thompson thinks she's for real, and he's been keeping tabs on her for a few months now. I've only met her once, but I think Cliff's right."

"I saw that in the report. But here's the other piece. And I'm not sure why I think they're linked, but it just smells that way to me. I ran across a completely unrelated bit from our embassy in Athens. Some low-level, low-life wannabe Greek Marxist got himself killed by his girlfriend."

"Lovers quarrel?"

"Sort of, but better than usual. She was cooking Easter dinner for him when they got into a beef. He heads out the door, and she chucks the dinner at him."

"He got killed by an Easter dinner?"

"This particular Easter dinner happened to be lamb on a spit. The spit caught him square in the chest. Right into his heart. The M.E. said he was probably dead before he hit the ground! You believe that shit?"

They both laugh like they're sharing an old joke.

"That's great stuff, but I don't see the connection."

"Our dead boyfriend was on the local radar given his Marxist leanings, so the Athenian constabulary searched his apartment pretty thoroughly after he was killed. They found a couple of old tickets for Crete with some Russian written on the back side. Turned them over to our embassy, and they sent them our way. Good police work there."

"So you think the Russian strike at the West Malenkov blabbed about could involve Crete?"

"Not involve Crete; it *is* Crete. It's perfect for the Sovs. Gives them essentially a naval fortress in the Eastern Med and control of everything from the Straits to the Suez."

Nick sits silently for a minute as he absorbs Arnold's theory.

"Crete's a tough nut to crack. Even the Nazis took their lumps during the occupation. Got anything else pointing that way?"

"Not a thing. That's it. And I might just be seeing ghosts here where none exist. It's more than thin, but I tell you what, Nick, there's something there. I can absolutely feel it."

"I might have something."

"Shoot."

"KRIPO was tracking a load of contraband flying out of Istanbul and headed for Berlin. The flight never made it. It started falling out of the sky east of Crete, did a 180 at the coast, over a pretty remote spot, recovered altitude and went back to Istanbul."

"When was this?"

"Back in April."

"Anyone check it out when it landed?"

"Air Force and C.D. Simon, our man in Istanbul. Nothing unusual. Weights and cargo all checked out. Engine trouble, according to the crew."

"Engine trouble my ass. That was a drop or my name's not Bob Arnold."

"Makes sense. The manifests are easy enough to fake, and things are pretty loose there in Istanbul. Might just be smugglers."

"Or supplies for an insurgent cell. Didn't you guys turn an old German Navy man a couple of months back? Maybe he's got something for us."

"Too late."

"How's that?"

"D.O.A., and he didn't leave a will, so to speak. No papers, no docs, nothing that could help us out, at least not that we found."

"Shit. But he's navy. Could be he put something together that the Sovs couldn't risk getting out."

"It's a stretch, but it fits your theory."

"Well, if I'm right about this thing, no one's gonna just walk into your office and say, 'Here's the plan!' They'll have things buttoned up even tighter than usual."

"And he took a round in the squash before he could squawk. That fits too. Anyone talk to the Greek girlfriend yet?"

"No. That's the next step. You want to volunteer?"

"Greece is out of my bailiwick, and I'm not a fan of flying, lethal lamb."

Arnold lets out a deep, hearty laugh.

"Well, I doubt she's a repeat offender. As far as Greece goes, it's right up your alley if the Russians are sticking their noses into it."

"True enough."

"She's got a university education, so her English should be solid. Why not? Get a trip to Athens out of it."

"You in a hurry on this?"

"Not really. The Porter woman said a year. So, next spring is what we're looking at if there's anything here. Given that we've seen nothing but these bits and pieces, it feels like we have time. Probably just a batch of coincidences, but I think it's worth taking a closer look."

"All right. I'll put Athens on my list. We're here in the States for another two weeks, and then it's back to Berlin. I'll send our Olympic javelin thrower a wire."

"Perfect. Let's talk about what you should ask her."

"How 'bout over lunch. I'm buying."

"Absolutely."

With that, two of the best analytical minds in the CIA head out of the building at 2430 E Street NW for what would look to any observer to be nothing more than another casual Washington, D.C., business lunch.

CHAPTER 20

A STATESIDE SECESSION

The phone rings in Nick's Statler Hotel room in Washington, D.C. He finishes rinsing the remaining shaving cream off his face, grabs a hand towel, walks into the bedroom, and picks up the phone.

"Hello."

He dries his face as he listens.

"Long distance for Mr. Nick Temple."

"Go ahead, operator."

"Your party is on the line, ma'am."

"Ellie?"

"Yes, Nick. It's me."

"Where are you? I'm supposed to meet your flight in an hour? Did you miss your plane out of Boston?"

"We didn't get on."

"Sounds like you're on vacation time. No sweat. Take a later flight. You got a flight number so I'll know when to pick the three of you up?"

"We're not getting on a flight. We're not going back to Berlin."

"Change of plans?"

"Nick, you don't understand. We're not ever going back to Berlin."

"What? All three of you?"

"I've enrolled the kids at Kent and Rosemary Hall. We're staying on the Cape until school starts. I'll go to my sister's in San Marino then."

"Are you kidding? Is this a joke?"

As Nick asks, he can't help thinking that a year in the legendary Bill Armstrong's classroom at Kent wouldn't be such a bad thing for his son.

"No, Nick. I can't go back to Berlin. There's nothing for me there."

"Nothing for you? What about the kids? Our lives together? What about you and me? That's nothing?"

"You're never home. It's almost as bad as the war. The kids and I will be together, so nothing will really change there. They're sick of Berlin, too. It's hard on them. They're always nervous. It's not a good place, especially for children. I suppose it's a good place for spies, so I doubt you've noticed."

"Don't you think we should have talked about this a little first? Don't I have any say in where the kids are? What's best for them? Where we live?"

"Dan works at the RAND Corporation in Santa Monica. Ruthie said he could probably get you on there. A lot of intel types are signing on. You could too, Nick."

"Fuck Dan, and fuck California. I've got a job. A damn good job and a damn important job. I don't need a new goddamn job! Are you asking me for a divorce?"

"No, Nick. Just a change."

"I don't know what to say, Ellie. I can't just pick up and leave. You know that. It's not that kind of job. You knew that when we signed on for Berlin."

"You have to make a choice, Nick. You have our address here. I'll be at Ruthie's in San Marino by the end of September after the kids get settled at their new schools. I want you to be with us. I want us all to be together, for once. But I can't go back to Berlin. Good bye, Nick."

"Wait. Can't we talk about this a little more? Can't . . ."

"Good bye, Nick."

Nick holds onto the receiver long enough to hear a dial tone. Stunned, he sets the receiver in his lap for a minute before hanging up. The man who has accurately predicted nearly every major move by the Soviet Union for more than a decade never saw this one coming.

CHAPTER 21

BEYOND SABRE RATTLING

In 1954, the age of massive armies driving relentlessly across vast stretches of Europe and North Africa seems to have given way to the age of the hydrogen bomb, a weapon so destructive that its very existence makes serious men use words like Armageddon and apocalypse. Mechanized corps, tank armies, and airborne divisions seem almost quaint in the face of the new destructive forces scientists and politicians have unleashed. Some strategic planners on both sides of the Iron Curtain recognize the possibility that the next major conflict will not be decided by the face-to-face slaughter that characterizes the engagement of conventional ground forces. They envision, instead, raining the newest weapons of mass destruction down on the enemy as quickly, as thoroughly, and as indiscriminately as possible. Others disagree, arguing that the newest weapons are so frightening that no nation can actually contemplate using them; therefore, the ability to put into the field mobile and massive conventional forces remains not only relevant but decisive.

Lost in the noise created by this debate is the strategic application of small units of highly trained commandos. While most military strategists view such units as having tactical value, those who understand the nature of nationalist struggles against colonialism and dictatorial struggles against insurgencies know small teams of men used with surgical precision can ignite a spark that cannot be extinguished, a spark that can move a small but strategically vital nation from one camp to another; that such teams may be all the force needed to tip a small and fragile nation one way or the other and thus affect the balance of world power; that such teams are not only relevant, but may represent the greatest bang for the buck the Superpowers can hope to obtain in their quest for geopolitical advantage.

The possible strategic importance of such teams is what drew Yuri Shevardnadze to them when he was a young Soviet Army officer. While others sought conventional commands, Shevardnadze was convinced that volunteering to serve in the Soviet Union's Spetsnaz GRU, its elite special forces, gave him his best shot at participating in game-changing, high stakes action in the service of his country. Two weeks ago the orders setting a process in motion that could make Shevardnadze's dream a reality came down. The highly unusual move of having the Strike Team under his command attached to the Black Sea Fleet confirms for the young Captain that influential voices in the Kremlin share his vision.

Tonight, in a hangar in Morozovsk, he and the 39 other men of Strike Team Two inspect and assemble their gear in preparation for their transfer. The Captain has enough experience to know that he and his men are about to undergo a level of training few will ever encounter and they will then be ordered to put their lives on the line for their country. The young Captain's heart swells with pride as he contemplates his glorious future.

CHAPTER 22

NICK GOES SOLO

Four weeks, ten letters, six telegrams, and a handful of pointless phone calls after being told by his wife that she and their children would not be part of his life anymore unless he quits the most important job he's ever had, Nick Temple fixes himself another dinner of scrambled eggs. In all of the years he spent in college, in the Army, in the OSS, and in the CIA, he never once learned to cook. His diet these days consists of breakfasts of cold cereal, lunches of Turkish donor kebabs from an Imbiss stand two blocks from work, and dinners of either grilled cheese sandwiches or scrambled eggs. In short, his diet's a mess; his clothes are a mess; his bathroom's a mess, his kitchen's a mess; and the rest of his house would be a mess too if he made any use of it. He doesn't.

When Nick walks into the office the next morning, he does so having decided enough is enough. As soon as he hears his secretary come in to work, he buzzes her. She comes into his office with a pot of coffee.

"Terry. I need a Putzfrau, and I need one now."

"I'll get to work on it. And good morning to you, Mr. Temple," she says as she fills his cup with fresh, black coffee.

"Right, sorry, good morning. And make sure she does laundry. Is that possible?"

"Pay in dollars?"

"Absolutely."

"Then anything's possible."

"And find out what's running at the Deutsche Oper."

"Yes, Mr. Temple."

Terry leaves, closing Nick's office door behind her.

The feeling of having straightened his life out by dishing his problems to his secretary isn't quite as satisfying as he'd hoped it would be. After a moment's reflection he realizes that clean laundry and a night at the opera are no substitute for the stable family life he thought he had. The fact is that until the Cape Cod phone call from Ellie he rarely gave any thought to his family's stability. He's been so wrapped up in the foreign policy problems of his country for so long that he has never been able to see the domestic problems of his family festering right under his nose. Nick is about to resolve to put in the effort necessary to rebuild his family life when the phone rings. He picks up the receiver.

"Mr. Durant from the NSA on line one."

Ted Durant is one of the good guys. While there are those at both CIA and NSA who see the two agencies as competitors, Ted and Nick see their roles as complimentary. They share a long range view that puts the good of the country well ahead of pointless bureaucratic squabbling.

Nick pushes the flashing button on his phone.

"Ted, thanks for returning my call."

And just like that, Nick Temple sets aside his thoughts of crumbling family and dives back into the Cold War.

By lunch Nick has a cleaning woman, the same woman the deputy commander of the Berlin Brigade uses, and two tickets to La Traviata for a week from Friday night. Today already beats the hell out of yesterday.

"Two tickets. Jesus. What was I thinking?"

He knows exactly what he was thinking, but he can't pull the trigger. He's got ten days to call Vanessa Porter and ask her if she'd be interested in accompanying him to dinner followed by a night at the opera. He thought about having Terry set it up like it was some sort of clandestine meet to go over the Malenkov file again, but that struck him as soon as he thought of it as chicken-shit in the extreme. He's also sure Vanessa Porter would see right through the pretense. Instead, he pulls the Porter file from his credenza, flips to Thompson's report, finds her phone number and dials. No sense putting it off. Besides, if she declines the invitation he may need ten days to find someone willing to accompany him.

"Porter, hier."

"Mrs. Porter. It's Nick Temple."

"Good afternoon, Mr. Temple. How nice to hear from you."

"How are you?"

"I'm quite well, thank you. What can I do for you?"

"You can accompany me to dinner followed by La Traviata at the Theater des Westens a week from Friday."

A moment of silence follows during which about a thousand ridiculous thoughts go through Nick's head.

"Can I assume there are no personal barriers to such an evening?" she asks discreetly.

"You can. I'll explain over dinner if you'll allow me."

"I'm more than willing to listen."

"Fine. I have your address. I'll pick you up at your apartment at six then."

"Six it is. Thank you, Mr. Temple."

"Please, call me Nick,"

"We shall see, Mr. Temple. Until next Friday."

As he hangs up he realizes he never gave his morning's resolution a chance, and he tells himself that it probably doesn't matter.

CHAPTER 23

HOUSEKEEPING SOVIET STYLE

Three men wait silently on the small wharf of the harbor at Agios Nikolaos. Although the sun has been down for hours, the early autumn night is still warm. The men chain smoke, nervously checking their watches by moonlight as they wait for the fishing boat to take them to Agioi Pantes a few hundred meters out in Mirabello Bay.

At just before midnight, the bow lights of a small fishing boat creep towards them. As the boat pulls slowly into the harbor, its bow lights flash three times, the prearranged signal. The men put their cigarettes out and wait for the boat to come alongside the wharf.

A crew member tosses a spring line to the men. The tallest of the three grabs it and secures it to a bollard on the wharf. A man dressed from head to foot in black steps off the boat and onto the wharf. He addresses them in their native Greek.

"Where is the fourth?"

"Dead."

"How?"

"An accident on Easter Sunday. It's not worth going into."

"You should have reported it."

"It's not important. He wasn't committed. It's probably for the best."

"Anyone else on the trip?"

"His girlfriend, but she didn't hear a thing."

"You're certain?"

"Politics doesn't interest her. She's a shallow woman. You needn't worry."

"Okay. Get on board. We'll go over the details when we get to Agioi Santes."

The crewmember and two of the men from the wharf step onto the boat immediately. The third removes the spring line from the bollard, throws the line to the helmsman, and jumps on board just before the boat backs away from the wharf.

When the harbor's fairway is sufficiently wide, the helmsman turns the boat 180 degrees and heads towards the bay. Once clear of the harbor, the boat accelerates and maintains its speed as it quickly approaches and then bypasses Agioi Pantes.

One of the men from the wharf speaks up.

"Where are we going? Why isn't he stopping?"

As if on cue, two men, both armed with fully loaded AK-47s come up from the small cabin under the bow. The first one orders the three men to stand at the stern of the boat. They comply.

"What the hell are you doing?"

"Moscow thanks you for your invaluable service."

The two armed men open fire, nearly emptying two 30-round clips into Niko Lendaris' hapless co-conspirators. The force from the barrage sends the three riddled, lifeless bodies overboard at which point the firing stops. Executioners and crew, switching to Russian, complement each other on a job well done as the fishing boat heads out to the open water of the Sea of Crete on its way to the Aegean. They'll have plenty of time to scrub their victims' blood off the boat's deck and transom before the sun comes up.

CHAPTER 24

AN ITALIAN LESSON

The small, second floor restaurant can seat no more than 30 people comfortably at its ten tables. For the most part, the tables are occupied by couples. Nick and Vanessa sit at a table against the window overlooking Berlin's Kantstrasse, three blocks from the Theater des Westens. The curtain goes up on La Traviata in two hours giving them plenty of time to eat and stroll leisurely to the theater.

Nick reads the menu with the aid of the flame from a small candle in the neck of an empty burgundy bottle on their table. When he chose the restaurant it did not occur to him that the menu might be in a language he does not read.

"My French is terrible," he admits.

Vanessa finds the admission charming; she offers her assistance.

"I can help."

Nick turns his menu so she can see it.

"Show me where the chicken livers are. I don't want to order chicken livers."

Vanessa points to the "foies de poulet" half way down Nick's menu.

"Have you tried them here?"

"I've never tried them here or anywhere. They just don't sound like food to me."

"Maybe if you'd only ever heard their French name."

"Maybe."

"How's your Italian?"

"Not much better. Solid English, German and Russian. The least romantic of Europe's languages, I'm afraid."

"But you're an admirer of Verdi?"

"It's terrible, I know. I don't understand a word, but I love Italian opera. It's the music that does it for me. Sounds foolish, doesn't it?"

"I'm relieved."

"Relieved?"

"After your call I'm afraid I read too much into your invitation."

"I don't understand."

"La Traviata. Do you know what it means?"

"I don't have a clue. I always assumed it was someone's name."

"It means 'the fallen woman.'"

"You have my word I meant nothing by the invitation other than hoping for a chance to enjoy dinner and the opera with a charming companion."

"Of course."

Nick looks around. The evening is not off to the start he envisioned.

"Where's our damn waiter? I'm going to need a drink."

As he looks across the tables of the small restaurant he sees a familiar face, the wife of a Berlin Brigade staff officer. She is dining with a teenage girl, probably her daughter. She looks away when Nick's glance catches hers, and any hopes Nick harbored that his evening with Vanessa would stay private evaporate.

CHAPTER 25

THE MISSING LINK?

Cliff Thompson has heard it before. Everyone has something to sell the Americans: stateside cigarettes, real coffee, high-end liquor, women, children, information. The Americans have what everyone wants: dollars. Germany was at one time the intellectual and industrial center of continental Europe. But after the war its battered and forlorn people were practically reduced to begging just to survive. Throw a currency backed by the world's unquestioned western Superpower into the mix, and the results are fairly predictable.

Thompson usually isn't buying. His experience tells him he can find the man who has something to sell him. The man who comes to him with something to sell usually has nothing more than a pile of shit wrapped in a hard luck story that isn't worth an East German pfennig.

But this East German courier is different. He's a civilian translator working at the Soviet Union's 5th Shock Army HQ in Berlin. He found his way to Thompson through a circuitous route that involved a hooker, a retired Air Force Sergeant, an auto shop mechanic, and a taxi driver. All in a day's work. His story, at least the snippet he was willing to give Thompson during their meet in Kreuzberg, fits together with the intel from the Porter woman. He claims he has documentary evidence of a Soviet military adventure planned for next spring. Thompson has to look into it, so the second meet, the delivery, is scheduled to start in under a minute, at precisely 2200 hours, local time.

Thompson walks out of the shadow of an alley just off of Unter den Linden. He lights a cigarette, takes a single puff and throws it to the ground before crushing it with his shoe. Moments later, the courier appears, a slight, beady-eyed man whose thin moustache twitches as he talks.

"Walk with me," Thompson commands.

They begin to walk away from Unter den Linden.

"Where are the docs?"

"Not here."

"That's bullshit. We're through!"

"No, I have them. I'm certain I'm being followed," the courier pleads.

"That's not my concern. You want the money, you come through with the documents. It's simple."

"Okay, okay. But not here."

"Where? One last chance. I ought to put a bullet in your skull right here."

"On the Wannsee."

"What?"

"Five hundred meters due east of the German-British Yacht Club."

"You're out of your mind."

"It's the only place safe. You want the docs, you'll be there."

"No place is safe. When?"

"Eleven at night. Thursday."

"Last chance."

"I know. Bring the money."

"You'd better use it to buy a plane ticket to some rat hole that doesn't interest your Soviet masters. You know you're a dead man, right?"

"I can take care of myself."

"Sure you can, Pee Wee."

"What? Who?"

"Never mind. See you Thursday. Last chance."

Thompson stops, turns and walks quickly back towards Unter den Linden.

"Nick's not gonna like it," he thinks to himself. "Hell, I don't like it."

The trembling courier looks after Thompson for a moment before scampering off into the night.

CHAPTER 26

NIGHT FISHING

A light, cold rain falls as Nick Temple fuels a small cabin cruiser tied to a wharf just north of Potsdam. Cliff Thompson stows a duffle bag containing a selection of automatic weapons, loaded ammunition clips, and a bag of American dollars under the floorboards of the v-berth just forward of the wheelhouse. They don't expect trouble, but just in case, they'll be ready. Their 2300 hours rendezvous point is 500 meters due east of the German-British Yacht Club, a point in the middle of the Wannsee, the vast lake that borders Berlin to the southwest. Two more weeks and the lake could easily be frozen over. For now it's navigable.

At this late hour, the Wannsee will be nearly deserted. The cold rain reduces the chance of an unwelcome encounter to almost zero. Nick thinks the meet is far too much cloak and dagger bullshit, but the courier made the call. Nick knows if he wants the docs he'll have to play along. When Cliff Thompson brought the set up to Nick, he volunteered to tag along – one more reason for Nick to wonder if the guy is stable.

He finishes fueling and tells Thompson to start the engine. Just as the boat's small diesel engine turns over and begins idling, a flashlight shines in Nick's eyes. An officious East German inspector decides to see who is going boating at this hour of a rain-soaked night.

"Was gibt's hier?"

Nick decides to be aggressive. These guys are either at your throat or at your feet. Might as well find out which it's going to be.

"Sprechen sie Englisch?"

"Ja."

"This operation is being conducted under direct orders of the Allied High Commission. Please stand clear of the vessel."

"High Commission? What kind of High Commission business are you conducting here at this hour?"

"You've no authority to interfere."

"Answer my question and produce some identification or I will be forced to impound this craft and take you in for questioning."

Thompson slides silently down into the forward berth toward the cache of weapons.

Nick gets out his Allied High Commission identification, the equivalent for years in post-war Germany of a get-out-of-jail free card.

"All right, here's my I.D. Now, I'm warning you. If you don't stand clear of the boat, you'll be shoveling dog shit in Düsseldorf for the rest of your life."

Nick can see Thompson out of the corner of his eye armed and ready to let the nosey inspector have it. Nick waves him off with a slight gesture of his right hand.

The inspector shines his flashlight on Nick's identification and then briefly on Nick's face to ensure the two match. His attitude changes immediately.

"Of course. Apologies, sir. Let me help you cast off. Are you sure you have everything you need for your trip? I'll stand by. Here, no need for you to do that. I'll cast you off. No need to report any of this, is there, sir?"

"From the throat to the feet in record time," Nick thinks to himself.

"Just stand clear. I'll take it from here," he orders.

"Of course, sir."

The inspector obeys, bowing slightly as he backs up. Nick feels sure the inspector would click his heels and go into a hearty "Heil Hitler" if prompted. Nick actually feels bad for the guy – just some poor schmuck trying to survive in a brutal world that keeps chewing up and spitting out endless loads of poor schmucks.

Thompson comes out of the companionway's shadow to stand behind the boat's wheel. Nick casts off the bow line and gives the small cruiser's nose a shove before hustling to the stern line. He casts off the stern line and hops aboard as Thompson flips a switch turning on the bow, stern and binnacle lights, engages the engine, eases on the throttle, and cuts the wheel to starboard. The boat heads slowly for the broadest part of the black, cold Wannsee.

As they approach the rendezvous point, Thompson switches on a small searchlight on the wheelhouse roof. He cuts the engine to idle and glides with just enough headway to maintain steerage.

"There. Off the port bow," Nick almost whispers.

Thompson cuts the wheel to starboard and puts the engine in reverse to halt the boat's progress. He shines the light on a small launch now off their port beam. A man, his feet and hands bound, his throat slit, his face bruised and swollen from a vicious beating, his dead eyes open wide in eternal terror, lies lifeless across the launch's two wooden benches.

"Your courier?" Nick asks.

"Looks like I'll need a new one. Want to get him aboard?"

"No dice. He's probably booby trapped. Let's get the fuck out of here."

As Nick scrambles below for firepower, Thompson kills the boat's lights, throws the engine into forward, and opens up the throttle. He cuts the wheel hard to starboard. Suddenly, the courier's body explodes. Thompson is momentarily blinded by the flash, but certain there's no other traffic on the lake, he brings the wheel back to stop his turn and leaves the engine at full throttle. Gunfire can be heard above the engine.

Nick comes up from below armed with a Sten Mk V submachine gun. He returns fire over the port gunwale with three-round bursts. A round shatters a window on the port side of the wheel house and catches Thompson's left hand.

"Son of a bitch!" Thompson shouts.

Nick continues to fire. He drops an empty clip and reloads. Two more rounds slam into the bow well above the water line before the firing stops.

Nick looks at Johnson's wound.

"First aid down below. I'll take us out of here."

Nick slings the smoking weapon over his shoulder and takes the wheel as Thompson heads below.

Nick flips on the binnacle light and heads east by southeast. After another minute, he turns on the bow and stern lights. Thompson reappears from below with his hand wrapped.

"You all right?"

"Yeah. I think it was nearly spent. Just caught some flesh. No bone. Back to Potsdam?"

"No. I'm taking us to the American boathouse. If that German inspector heard the explosion and gunfire, he'll probably call for reinforcements. No sense getting back in his face, especially with the damage to the boat. I'll see if I can raise them on the radio. If anyone's guarding the boathouse, I'll make sure we're cleared coming in."

"I wonder what he had for us."

Nick pauses for a minute to ponder the events of the last 60 seconds.

"It must have been big. The Sovs aren't given to subtlety, but I haven't seen that clear of a 'Don't fuck with us' message since the war. We're onto something, my friend. No doubt about it. We're getting closer to whatever Ivan's got up his sleeve. But Bob Arnold was right. No one's going to deliver it to us in a neatly wrapped package."

Nick eases back on the throttle and steadily, quietly glides through the near-freezing rain of the Wannsee, his new destination the dock at the American Armed Forces recreation area on the east side of the lake.

"Take the wheel. I'm going to check the boat for body parts before I work the radio. No sense docking with a stray hand or foot sloshing about in the bilge."

Thompson takes the wheel. Nicks goes forward to retrieve a flashlight as he mutters to himself, "Too much cloak and dagger bullshit."

CHAPTER 27

GREETINGS FROM PASADENA

Terry delivers the morning mail and newspapers to Nick whose focus is on the daily SIGINT, signals intelligence, briefing from NSA. After setting the pile of paper on his desk, she freshens his coffee. She remains standing in front of his desk, coffee pot in hand. He barely notices her presence as he scours a report profiling the comms of the key leaders of a recent spate of student unrest in Berlin. He finally looks up as he reaches for his coffee cup.

"Something else?"

"Make sure you read your mail this morning, that's all."

Nick puts the report down. Once he turns his attention to the pile of mail, Terry turns and leaves, closing Nick's office door behind her.

On top of the pile is a thick letter from Ellie. He realizes they haven't had any contact for more than two months. It looks thick enough to be a summons and a petition for a divorce.

Nick takes a deep breath and opens the envelope. It's just a letter, a fact that's somewhat disappointing. He counts the pages–six handwritten–before he reads a word. He notices with some surprise that she still addresses him as "Dear Nick."

The letter starts out with some generic news about Ellie's sister and her sister's family. For a few weeks after Ellie moved to the West Coast, she would fill up half of her letters talking about her brother-in-law's great job in Santa Monica. Nick was not impressed. After reading for the third time about how Dan gets to spend all day in an air conditioned office, Nick thought to himself, "I'd rather clean toilets with my face than do what he does." Coincidentally, Ellie never mentioned Dan's job again. Nick still wonders if he made the "toilets with his face" remark aloud during one of their awkward long-distance phone calls.

After the news about her sister and brother-in-law, Ellie goes on to talk about how she's "adjusting" to her new life. Nick's sure she's laying it on pretty thick to make him feel like he's missing out on some swell times there in Southern California. Great weather, great beaches, lots of new friends. What's not to like? Berlin's weather and social life are easy targets making Ellie's nearly two pages about the sunshine, beaches, and new acquaintances feel like a cheap shot. No doubt her social life is hopping, thanks to Ruthie and Dan. He gets the feeling his in-laws have already written him off as a lost cause, and are focused on finding someone to take Ellie off their hands.

She saves chewing him out for being an "absentee husband and father" for the last couple of pages. None of it has much effect as he's heard and read it all before. The litany of his offenses, particularly during their time in Berlin, is familiar and more than a little tiresome until she slips in, "At least write to the kids." Even though his last two letters to each went unanswered, he knows she's right. He has to keep trying, at least when it comes to his children. And that thought surprises him – he realizes he is no longer interested in trying where his wife is concerned.

Ellie finishes her letter with a plea for him to remember how much they've meant to each other, and to put at least as much effort into saving their marriage as he puts into doing his job.

Nick sets the letter on his desk, rubs his temples and leans back in his chair. He is lost in a series of conflicted thoughts about his deepening relationship with Vanessa Porter when he hears a light knock on his door.

"Yeah."

Terry comes in with the coffee pot.

"Ready for more?"

"No, thanks."

"Still married?"

"Technically."

"Why not take the rest of the day off? Get out of the office. Do something fun."

Nick smiles. His secretary's concern is touching.

"Does that sound like me?"

"Just a thought."

She starts to leave the office.

"Terry?"

She turns back towards him.

"Yes, Mr. Temple?"

"Thanks for checking."

Terry smiles.

"Arnie in yet?"

"About 15 minutes ago."

"You know if he has anything going on today?"

"He doesn't."

"Great. Tell him I need to see him after lunch and that he should clear his calendar for the rest of the day."

"Yes, Mr. Temple."

As Nick tries to focus on the work ahead of him, he realizes that once again Ellie's letter makes no mention of Vanessa or his evening out with her. He wonders if the staff officer's wife who saw them out together is being discreet or has kept the information to herself all of these weeks while she settles on a strategy.

CHAPTER 28

STAYING ON A COLD TRAIL

Nick Temple and Arnie Miller, ties loosened, collar buttons undone, sleeves rolled up, sit in Nick's office where files, maps, memos, and coffee mugs cover Nick's desk. It's closing in on midnight, but neither one of them gives a thought to the time. They're back on Bob Arnold's Crete theory; they can't let it go even though its looks for all intents and purposes like there was nothing there in the first place, that they were all seeing connections that don't exist. The late night session continues, neither man willing to give up.

"What are we missing, Arnie?"

"Look, if Bob Arnold can't nail it, maybe it, whatever it is, just isn't there."

"Let's go over it one more time."

"All right by me."

"Take them in order."

Arnie opens the TOP SECRET file on his lap, puts his feet on a pile of papers on Nick's desk, and begins to read. Nick clasps his hands behind his head, puts his feet up too, and stares at the ceiling as Arnie reads, flipping file pages as he goes back over the evidence acquired to date.

"March 3, Pravda and Izvestia hint at major move by Krushchev in articles on anniversary of Stalin's death, according to fortune teller and all around Soviet wizard, Mr. Nick Temple, and Bob Arnold agrees with said wizard; April 1, defecting former East German naval officer assassinated, Soviet Sector, brains in the back seat of his Pobeda, which is a serious upgrade to the car's interior; April 18, low life Marxist with travel record to Crete killed by his Easter dinner cooking girlfriend, who I plan to ask to marry me as soon as I meet her, by the way; April 28, flight from Istanbul to Berlin doubles back after what looks like a drop of nothing over a section of Crete where nobody lives; May 30, Vasily Malenkov's major OPSEC violation, which in case you didn't know is the key to this entire deal, delivered while he was so drunk that he can't remember any of it. Nice, rock-solid HUMINT, that; November 18, East German courier from 3rd Shock HQ murdered after offering to sell non-specific information to Americans. Probably deserved it. Body converted to fish food. That's it. That's what you and Bob think adds up to an imminent, major push by the Soviets in the Eastern Mediterranean. You don't know where. Maybe Crete, or maybe Lendaris was just another low-life Commie playing pretend revolutionary with his tiny little gang of nobodies. You don't know when. Maybe within a year. Maybe more. Maybe in the spring. No one seems to thinks the Sovs are ready. You don't know why. Control the Med? Control the Suez? Get the Egyptians on board? Control the Straits? Construct a resort or two for fat-cat Commies? All of the above? And you don't know who. In spite of the civilian contacts, no military SIGINT that we're aware of mentions any of the activity you're convinced makes up the plot. Soviet Navy? Nichego. Group of Soviet Forces Germany? Nichts zu melden. Soviet Air Force? Not a peep. No reports of high ranking officers making any FEBA visits other than the normal cycles, standard field exercises, and forward area inspections designed to harass soldiers and sailors whose lives are already miserable. You know, when I think about it, except for a couple of dead bodies here and there, it's been a pretty dull year, considering we're on the brink of Armageddon just about every day, at least according to you and Bob."

Arnie's quick wit and sarcasm are exactly what's needed at this hour. Nick smiles all the way through the report, even laughing out loud at points. When all is said and done, he has to admit, there ain't much there there. He opens his bottom right desk drawer, pulls out a bottle of contraband Irish Whiskey and two glasses, sets the glasses on a pile of papers on his desk, and pours two shots.

"Now we're getting somewhere," Arnie says as he rubs his hands together.

"Bottoms up, my friend. When all else fails, turn to alcohol! An old family motto."

They throw back the shots.

Nick is not willing to give up.

"Let's focus on what we're missing instead of what we have."

"Okay. We're missing everything. Next assignment?"

"Seriously. First, no specific location, but Bob's convinced it's Crete, but even if it is Crete, where on Crete? Second, no military traffic, but if Bob's right it's got to be a naval operation. Third, how do they take control of Crete if it is the target? What are the key political targets? The key hard targets?"

"Look, Nick, I don't think we're going to get anything fresh out of the traffic that's already been reported. Between D.C. and us, I can't believe that we've actually missed anything."

"We haven't, and that's the point. If we want the rest of the picture, we're going to have to shift to active mode. We've been sitting around working the traffic, digging through the docs, waiting for the phone to ring. It's time to work the problem from the outside."

"Well you're right about that. We haven't exactly been on the hunt. Got any ideas?"

"From here on out, we proceed on the theory that Crete's the target."

"Why not?" Arnie says as he pours himself another shot.

"I need to find out what Lendaris did on Crete. That's easy enough. I'll take another stab at getting his ex-girlfriend to talk to me. That's another trip to Athens. Not a problem. And I want to talk to Navy and Army intelligence. Let's bring in Ted Durant to get them focused on Crete, the Med, and the Black Sea. Tell them what we're looking for. Give their ops a heads up so they don't roll off something that looks harmless but might fit in. They can go back through their traffic, too. Maybe they've got something and don't even know it. At some point we need to get to Crete. Talk to whoever runs that Monastery, see if Bobs' right about the drop, see what we can get off the street, out of the papers. Really work the problem instead of just sitting here waiting for it to come to us."

"When do we start?"

Nick looks at his watch, stands up, and grabs his coats from his coatrack.

"First thing in the morning. That's enough for today. I'll check in with the comms center. You should head home."

"Don't have to tell me twice."

CHAPTER 29

A WIDER NET

Ted Durant's a lifer, no doubt about it. He's one of many in his generation who signed up to serve his country on December 8, 1941, and has been serving it ever since.

World War II interrupted his first career choice. Durant was sitting in his small office at Pomona College in Claremont, California, using the quiet Sunday morning to grade his calculus students' final exams when a colleague burst in to tell him about the attack on Pearl Harbor. Durant quietly finished grading the exams, submitted his grades and his resignation the next morning, and drove to an Army recruiting station in Los Angeles that afternoon.

He spent most of the war working in the European Theater in the Army's Signals Intelligence Division. His Ph.D. in applied mathematics made him a natural at analyzing and breaking out coded transmissions. The weapons he employed were a radio receiver, a pencil, a code book, and his remarkably lucid mind. His reputation as the Army's "go to guy" on cryptologic analysis stuck, and after the CIA was formed in 1947 he often found himself working side by side with his civilian counterparts in their D.C. headquarters. The Korean War put an end to his brush with office life; the Army needed his skills in another theater of combat. After Korea, he joined the newly formed National Security Agency. Its emphasis on signals intelligence and cryptologic analysis was a perfect fit. The NSA immediately sent him to Berlin to work with Berlin

Brigade's G2, and, on occasion, to provide support to other American intelligence activities in the former German capital.

The office work is starting to get to him. His years in the field came with an independence he cherished, the sort of independence that doesn't fit in well with the growing bureaucracy of the NSA. He's getting cabin fever, big time.

Nick knows Durant's deserved reputation in the intelligence community; he decides to turn to Ted for assistance as he tries to unravel the Soviet Union's intentions, if there are any, regarding Crete. After yesterday's session with Arnie, Ted Durant is the first man Nick thought to contact. As it turns out, Ted is free first thing this morning and can meet Nick at Berlin Brigade Headquarters.

Nick parks his Fiat on Hüttenweg, crosses to the east side of Clayallee and heads south towards Brigade HQ. He sees Durant standing to the north side of the entrance. Durant looks up and quickly heads Nick's way. Both men are dressed against the early morning cold of a late November day in Berlin. A light snow dusts the pervasive gray of the suburban landscape.

"Okay if we do this while we walk?" Durant asks.

"Not a problem. What happened, get your access pulled?"

Durant laughs.

"Nothing like that. I've got a whole day of goddamn meetings scheduled. I need to get back in the field. Too many meetings. Too much time indoors."

"Rather be out in this weather?"

"Any weather."

"Maybe we can help each other."

"What've you got?"

Nick looks around to see if they're being tailed. The sidewalk is empty in both directions.

"Bob Arnold and I have been working on something. It looks to us like the Sovs are going to make a big move next spring in the Eastern Med."

"Bob Arnold? He's usually rock solid. So what's the deal? Why haven't I heard about it?"

"We can't wrap it up. Not enough detail. Too much speculation. Too many unconnected dots."

"The Director in on this?"

"No. I'm as high as it goes for now. And I need some help."

"Fire away."

"If we're right about this thing, we should be seeing some kind of military comms at least hinting at a move. We haven't seen a thing."

"KGB?"

They come to Hüttenweg and turn right, away from Nick's car.

"Operationally, it's probably too small for them, but that's a guess. I need you to get word out to the services, but it has to be discreet. We're looking for any training exercises out of the ordinary. Maybe small units deployed by the Black Sea Fleet. Maybe paratroopers or commandos. Some sort of combined forces exercise, but not the typical massive field deployment Ivan loves. Small units, like I said."

"Spetsnaz?"

"That would surprise me considering the units they're usually attached to, but it's worth a look. It's critical to get the word out without tipping our hand. If D.C. gets ahold of this, the whole thing is liable to spiral out of control."

"Don't trust the big boys?"

"It's not really a trust issue. Their perspective is too global. This thing smells like the Sovs are looking to score big without a lot of firepower, without a lot of noise. They're not shuffling any big units around so far as we can tell. They start that action and it'll be off my desk in a minute. But right now, it feels covert, so KGB might fit. If we're right about that, then our best response is covert, not the 82nd Airborne and the 1st Armored Cav."

"I'll see what I can do."

"I'd appreciate it."

Durant stops walking.

"I'll walk you to your car."

"I'm a couple of blocks back down Hüttenweg."

They reverse direction and head towards Nick's car retracing their visible footprints in the snow.

"Now what were you going to do for me?"

"We might need a crypto guy to handle the field intercept if we put an operation together. Interested?"

"Time out of the office?"

"Guaranteed."

"Hell yes, I'm interested."

"NSA have any problem attaching you to my office?"

"I'm sure there's some load of paperwork that you'll have to fill out. Let's see if it comes to that."

"All right. You're in. Honestly, I hope we're wrong about this whole deal."

"Honestly . . . I hope you're right. I could use the tune up. Gotta go. I'll let you know if I hear anything."

Nick and Ted shake hands. Ted walks back to HQ; Nick heads for his car. He needs to go home and pack for Athens to take another crack at meeting up with Mika Ioannou.

CHAPTER 30

WHY NOT ON A SUNDAY?

Nick Temple wasn't sure what to expect when he left Berlin for Athens for the second time. The reports of both the Athenian police and the American Embassy forwarded to him by Bob Arnold back in D.C. contained no follow up questions about the two tickets found in the apartment of the late Niko Lendaris. After a pair of unproductive phone calls to a couple of uncooperative bureaucrats, and after his extended chat with Bob Arnold when he was in D.C., Nick decided to travel to Athens to interview Lendaris's killer himself.

His first visit was a bust. After finally tracking down the subject at work, she was clearly too busy to talk to him. She snuck away as he waited in front of her building for her, and Nick felt like an idiot. Twenty-four year old Greek beauty gives veteran spymaster the slip. No doubt she wasn't in a talking mood. Her response to his recent cable indicates a possible change of heart. It's certainly worth a try, so his visit begins early on a Sunday morning. After a quick hop from Tempelhof to Athens, he finds the apartment of Mika Ioannou, knocks on the door, and waits.

"Ti esti; (Who is it?)" a groggy female voice calls from the inside.

"My name's Nick Temple. I sent you a wire. Remember?"

"Who?"

"Nick Temple. I'm an American. You said we could talk this time."

Nick hears nothing for a moment and thinks Mika has simply gone back to bed. The door opens. A young woman, freshly out of bed and wearing nothing other than a long t-shirt, walks towards the small kitchen table leaving Nick to find his way in.

"I'm having coffee. Would you like a cup?" Mika offers without looking back at him.

Nick enters and takes a look around. A typical European studio that barely has room for the two of them and the basics: a bed that doubles as a couch, a small coffee table littered with magazines and an ashtray, a bookshelf filled to overflowing, a floor lamp, and a linoleum covered table with two chairs in the middle of a tiny kitchen. Even at this early hour the apartment is filled with December sunlight from its two thin windows.

"Sure, if it's not any trouble."

"None."

"On second thought, I'm not sure I should."

She stops and turns to look at this American she has just let into her apartment: late thirties, a touch of gray at the temples, serious without being grave.

"Why not? Really, it's no trouble."

"I hear your cooking can be deadly."

Mika bursts out laughing.

"Only if you act like a fool. Then watch out for flying objects!"

"Thanks for the safety tip. Okay, sure, I'll have a cup of coffee."

Nick has a seat at the kitchen table while Mika busies herself with getting grounds and water into the percolator.

"Your English is remarkable."

"We all learn English now. Languages are easy for me."

"It shows."

"What do the Americans want to know about me? The Athenian Police already cleared me. Lucky for me they hate Marxists. I think I could shoot Niko in the head in the middle of the Acropolis and not go to jail."

Mika sits down and crosses her bare legs. Her t-shirt supplies the barest hint of modesty.

"The two of you ever travel?"

"Only once. To Crete."

Nick offers Mika a cigarette. He was hoping she had accompanied Niko. His return trip to Athens is starting to look up.

"Thank you. No."

"How long were you there?"

"We were supposed to be there for a week. You know, some time on the beach, love making back at the hotel. Tourists living the good life. But we ended up leaving after three days. Niko got seasick on a boat to Santorini, and we left the next day."

"Were you traveling alone?"

"Sure. Just the two of us."

"Meet up with anybody once you got there?"

Mika gets up from the table.

"Coffee's ready."

She pours them each a cup of fresh coffee. She hands Nick his cup. She remains standing, holding her cup in her hands.

"Sugar? Milk? I'm afraid I can't get cream."

"No thanks. Black is fine. It smells great."

"What is the question?"

"Did the two of you meet up with anyone on Crete?"

"Not me. But Niko runs into some of his ridiculous Marxist friends. Five or six of them. I can't remember."

"Did you know any of them?"

"Never see them before or since."

"Any names?"

"Sure. The usual. You know, Demetrios, Yannis, Kostas. Maybe more."

"Last names?"

"They never say. They behave like schoolboys playing a silly game. Lots of whispering, sideways glances, looking over their shoulders. Just too ridiculous. I don't blame them, though."

"No?"

"Our government does not hesitate to arrest what they consider radical elements. Surely you know this."

"There's a lot of that going around. Was Niko a radical?"

Mika laughs once again.

"Not close. He used politics for sex, but he gets caught in his own trap."

"Caught?"

"He has to play along when these other comical Marxists sought him out. He hated it. I like to tease him about it, because I know it is all a charade with him. Just a way to get girls in his bed. It usually worked."

"One meeting, two, more?"

"Two times. Once they meet in the hotel lobby and then go outside. I guess they are afraid I hear their secrets and report them. The second time they meet across the street from some building in Mournies. They keep staring at it and whisper to each other. That was it. Half an hour of staring at a building and whispering about it. I can't imagine why Niko takes me on this trip. Great vacation, right?"

"The second building was near Souda?"

"Right. You know a lot about Crete?"

"Just a guess. Any other meetings?"

"That's it. We try to get to Santorini the next day. The sea is pretty rough, and the harbor master orders us back to Heraklion, but not before Niko spends an hour or more vomiting in front of his girlfriend. Really pathetic. How do you call yourself a Greek if you can't tolerate the sea?"

Nick finishes his coffee and gets up to go.

"Thank you so much for agreeing to talk to me. I hope you don't mind if I call on you again."

"Okay, but I'm not stupid. If the Americans are sending someone to talk to me about a dead rat like Niko, I must be missing something."

"It's probably nothing, just a way for me to spend a day in Athens talking to a barely dressed, beautiful young woman."

"Lucky you."

"One more question. Where was he when he caught his Easter dinner with his chest?"

Mika laughs and points to the door.

"Right there. He almost made it out. If he keeps walking instead of turning around, I miss him completely. Idiotic!"

"Regrets?"

"A perfectly good, and very expensive dinner wasted."

"She's tough," Nick thinks to himself as he closes the door behind him. "Tough and Greek. Just what the doctor ordered."

CHAPTER 31

HERE COMES SANTA CLAUS

Neither one of them expects much from Berlin's modest Christkindlmarkt. A stroll past a few booths strung with lights, a cup of hot glühwein, and a piece of apple strudel suffice. A light snow muffles the city's sounds and wraps the evening in a veil of momentary sanctuary. They find a dry bench under a canopy and finish their glühwein and strudel.

Christmas involves a mix of emotions for both of them. Nick spent Christmases during World War II overseas, separated from his young family as so many men of his generation were. Wives and children forgave those men for those important, if tortuous, years. The years after the war, when he was called away to attend to some duty or another on Christmas day, did more damage to his home life. The result is that he got used to anticipating the Christmas season with some regret, knowing the odds of once again disappointing his family were high.

Vanessa has not enjoyed Christmas since the brutal execution of her young, beautiful husband. Their lives together before the war seemed idyllic even then, and in retrospect they grow more idealized with the passing of each year. The war years were emotionally bleak, and each Christmas was worse than the one before it, serving only to remind her of how much she'd lost. She learned to ignore her personally joyless Christmas season, to treat it as any other time of year. Until now. A simple evening with the man she now shares her life with brings a warmth to her heart she hasn't experienced in years.

After another stroll around the market, they drive back to Nick's Lichterfelde house in near silence. The prospect of a night together fills their thoughts until they are nearly home when they both see the car parked across the street. This is the third time in a week that it's been there. Rather than bypassing the house and taking Vanessa home to her apartment again, Nick parks his car in the driveway. With an air of quiet defiance, he gets out of the car and goes around to open Vanessa's door. Together they head for the front door, their path illuminated by a street lamp as they ignore the man taking pictures from the car.

Nick unlocks the front door and lets Vanessa in ahead of him. He closes and locks the door behind him.

"Can you get a pot of coffee going? I'll be right back."

"What are you going to do?"

"Talk to our friend across the street."

"Don't shoot him. It could ruin an otherwise delightful evening."

"Not to worry."

Nick goes through the house and out the back door. He walks through neighborhood yards until he is two blocks down from his house. He walks half a block to his street, crosses to the far side and turns, heading back towards his house. He approaches the car from behind where there are no streetlights to give away his presence. He can see the man through the rear window sitting in the driver's seat still looking towards the front door of his house.

"Ellie's wasting my money on a private dick, and a lousy one at that," he thinks to himself as he pulls his Beretta M1951 out of its shoulder holster.

In one motion he opens the passenger door, slides into the car next to the private investigator, and sticks the Beretta against the investigator's temple.

"Merry Christmas, dickhead!"

"Was?"

"Sprechen sie Englisch?"

"Ja. Okay, okay. No shooting!"

"Look, asshole. Quit wasting my wife's fucking money, which just happens to be my money. I'll sign whatever you want that admits that everything you think about what I'm doing is true. Just stay the fuck away from my house. Got it?"

The trembling detective recovers long enough to blurt out, "Ja. Okay. Don't shoot. Okay!"

"Ask your German buddies about me. You knock this shit off, or you'll disappear and no one will give a fuck, got it?"

"Okay!"

Nick shoves the nose of the Beretta into the detective's neck just under his jaw.

"Now start the car."

"What?"

"Start the fucking car. Are you deaf?"

The detective starts the car.

"You have ten seconds to get out of range before I start firing."

"Okay! Okay! Don't shoot. I'm going!"

Nick gets out of the car and slams the door shut. The detective floors it, skidding in the fresh snow as he desperately speeds away from the crazy American.

Nick waits until the car is out of sight, holsters the Beretta and walks back across the street to his home where a hot cup of coffee awaits.

CHAPTER 32

PRACTICE MAKES PERFECT

It's an hour before dawn on a remote stretch of beach in the eastern Black Sea, northwest of Sochi. Six of the ten commandos from the last of Strike Team Two's four inflatables, dressed from head to foot in black, faces smeared with black grease, their assault rifles slung across their backs, carry their craft double time from the edge of the Black Sea's frigid surf towards the scrubby vegetation fifty meters in from the water. The other four men, divided into two groups of two men each, deploy on either side of the path from the sea, kneeling, their AK-47s at the ready to provide suppressing fire. Spetsnaz GRU SOP.

As the six men reach their deployment point with the inflatable, two of the four providing suppressing fire join them. The other two remain to guard the mission's rear flank. Eight commandos quickly remove the vessel's watertight satchels containing a field radio, thousands of 7.62 mm rounds, 8 pounds of plastique, and 16 sets of radio activated detonators. The rounds, plastique, and detonators are divided quickly and evenly among the men. The unit's radio operator does a quick comms check over his bulky R-129 indicating the unit's readiness to move inland. Team Two's three other units, spread out at 100 meter intervals down the beach, each with identical equipment and the identical number of men, respond to the comms check. Exactly ten seconds after the final unit's response, thirty-two commandos spread out along 300 meters of coastline move inland in unison.

A transmission from Captain Shevardnadze, the young commander of Strike Team Two comes over each of the unit's radios ordering the entire Team to stand down and regroup at the designated rendezvous point on the beach. Shevardnadze, while pleased with Team Two's progress over the last two months of near-constant drill, is certain they can shave up to 90 more seconds off their time from the order of deployment until readiness to move inland. Anything that increases their chance of complete tactical surprise is worth doing. He radios back to the Ognenny class destroyer *Bezboyaznenny*, the Fearless, waiting five kilometers offshore, that Team Two will be returning. He requests permission to repeat the drill once more before standing down for the night.

As he stands on the beach, waiting for a response to his request, Shevardnadze's mind turns to speculating about their ultimate target. No one on Team Two believes the drills are routine training. The drills' specificity and the interest Moscow has shown in the Team's progress can mean only one thing: the Team is training for a live mission of high import.

His musings are interrupted by a transmission from the *Bezboyaznenny* ordering the Captain to stand down the exercise given the impending dawn and return to the destroyer with the Team for a command debriefing. The Captain relays the order to the rest of Team Two. Without question, without hesitation, the Team's four units execute a flawless and swift return to the sea.

CHAPTER 33

BLACK SEA SECRETS

Staff Sergeant Chris Wilson lights a cigarette, puts his headphones back on, and decides to scan the HF range once more before his shift is over. He's cold as hell, as usual. His U.S. Army-issue field jacket seems designed to let the cold air in and his body warmth out. Two pairs of woolen socks under his combat boots can't keep his feet warm for the whole shift. At least his feet are dry, which makes Sinop better by far than Korea. And the cold keeps him awake, not that he'd miss anything by sleeping through another mid, what civilians call the graveyard.

The pass-on to the day whores–the shameless ass-kissers who somehow escape being assigned to mids–should be pretty straight forward again: nothing to report. Almost eight hours of static, a couple of Black Sea Fleet comms checks, and the usual miserable weather reports. Wilson can't figure out why the brilliant minds heading up the United States Army ever decided to stick elements of a Signal Corps unit on the godforsaken spit of land jutting into the Black Sea from Sinop, Turkey. In the first three months of his TDY assignment from Field Station Berlin, he's heard virtually nothing of interest. Turkey's decision to join NATO in 1952 sharply reduced the strategic significance of the Soviet Union's Black Sea Fleet, which is probably why Wilson is one of no more than 25 U.S. Army personnel still stationed at the post.

He glances at his watch. Ten more minutes. He aimlessly spins the dial on his receiver – "spinnin' and grinnin'," as they call it. On his last pass through the HF range he rolls over a signal that has a snippet of Russian voice in the clear. He stops, and rolls back until he picks it up again. Russian Navy, unencrypted. He hits the record button on his reel-to-reel, notes the time and frequency and continues to listen. Another burst of voice. Spetsnaz GRU! What the hell is this unit doing with the Black Sea Fleet? Naduvnye Lodki! Inflatable craft! Twelve of them, with ten men per boat. That's an entire company!

Wilson scribbles what he's able to pick up as his relief comes in. He takes a headphone off of one ear, and puts his cigarette out. Looking up, he notices his relief is in the intercept bay.

"Anderson, I've got Spetsnaz GRU at 8.6 megs at about 80 degrees. Dial it up and see if you can get the guy on the other end. He's in the clear, but I can hardly hear him."

Spec 4 Anderson isn't buying it.

"Come on, Sarge. Spetsnaz? Aren't they attached to tank brigades? Sinop duty's starting to get to you. Either that or a tank brigade is magically floating on the Black Sea. You choose."

Wilson ignores Anderson as he tries to find the signal again. The display on his screen goes flat for the entire HF range. After a minute of searching he reaches up, stops the recording, and takes off his headphones.

"Damn! They went down."

"You get them on tape?"

"You bet."

"All right. I'll transcribe it and get it to the analysts. You sure it's Spetsnaz?"

"Got their call signs in my hand copy. It's all on the tape."

"There was an Action Notice about unusual Black Sea traffic at Monday's briefing. You think this is what they were looking for?"

"Yeah. I remember. Could be. Let me know what you get. Have Burland sit on the frequency in case they come back up. I'm outta here. Time to catch some sleep."

Anderson sits down as Wilson heads for the drafty Quonset hut he'll unfortunately be calling home for three more months.

CHAPTER 34

ANOTHER PIECE

Bob Arnold sits in his office. It's nearly midnight, but his attention is once again squarely on Nick Temple's supplemental report not what time of day it is. He goes over it one more time. The details of Nick's visit to Athens are just enough to keep Arnold's thin theory from dying a slow, deserving death. Mika Ioannou's humorous recount of the low-level conspirators' secretive trip to Crete seems to confirm what the two men have been speculating about. The conclusions in Nick's report make sense, not surprisingly, but there's still not enough to sell it to anyone but each other. And even they have their doubts. They both know how important it is to guard against an investigator's tendency to interpret innocuous events as meaningful, particularly when the events fit a previously developed theory. It's the same tendency that causes an investigator to ignore facts that don't fit a theory, facts that might easily blow the theory apart. The bottom line is that if they go up the chain of command with what they have been able to put together to date, even with their combined reputations, they'll be dismissed as having let their collective imagination run a little too wild. Or, what's worse, their suspicions could cause the western world to foolishly overreact to a non-event putting a world already on edge that much closer to thermonuclear holocaust.

The news about a visit to Mournies is huge. The Greek Navy runs a radio station in Mournies and if someone, anyone, is interested in overthrowing a government, even one as dysfunctional as Crete's, capturing key command, control, and communication centers is vital. Mournies, just west of Crete's deep water port at Souda points to an amphibious assault from the north. Bob and Nick smelled a covert op a while back; a small-unit commando raid would be perfect for a strike aimed at Mournies via Souda. Niko and his gang were clearly interested in Mournies, but that's where the trail of hard evidence once again goes cold, and speculation takes over.

Like Temple, he can't decide if he is looking at a clumsy, amateurish plot that will go nowhere past heated, drunken declarations in some apartment filled with young, hapless Greek Communists, or the outlines of a bold move to be undertaken with the full military support of the Soviet Union to move Crete into the Soviet camp. Is the intel from the Porter woman solid? Or is it a coincidence? Or, worse yet, is it a plant, a diversion? If so, what is the real objective? Is Malenkov guilty of sloppy OPSEC, operational security? Or was he just trying to impress Porter with idle, drunken chit-chat? Why would a local KGB Operations Officer be in the loop on an Eastern Mediterranean thrust? Or is he in on the diversion? If it's not a coincidence, are the Soviets really relying on the late Niko Lendaris' low level conspirators? Are they a front, a head fake, puppets to be pushed aside when the Soviets achieve their objective? Who else would be able to afford an air drop from Istanbul? Or was that just a simple smuggling operation? Why hasn't he seen any chatter about Soviet units? The Black Sea Fleet? At least one of their Airborne Divisions if not a Corps? Why hasn't there been any traffic out of Sinop? Why haven't there been any unusual reports of high ranking officers moving to a potential forward area? Is he getting too old for this shit? Has he lost his touch? Is there some key scrap of information in one of the countless files on his desk that he's ignoring? And what, if anything, is he to make of the increased diplomatic traffic regarding May Day celebrations in Moscow? Is it just Krushchev solidifying his boda fides as the world's most important Commie? Are they building up to some big punch line? He's starting to feel like it's November 1941 all over again, and that if he doesn't get it right, the world is in for another cataclysm, the major difference being that this time around the hydrogen bomb has the potential to make World War II look like child's play.

He rubs his eyes and checks his watch for the first time in hours. He looks up and realizes that except for the trick trash–the moniker proudly worn by ordinary shift workers throughout America's vast intelligence community–monitoring overnight comms, he's nearly alone in the building. Bob Arnold, having done all he can for his country today, decides to go home.

Two minutes after Arnold leaves, his office phone rings. Nick Temple is on the secure line from Berlin anxious to relay the substance of a conversation he has just had with Ted Durant about an isolated fragment of SIGINT from Diogenes Station in Sinop, Turkey, on the southern edge of the Black Sea.

CHAPTER 35

RECRUITER'S CALL

Once Ben Sacolick has the connection to D.C. established Arnie and Nick pick up separate receivers for a conversation with Bob Arnold.

"Bob. I've got Arnie Miller here with me. He's been helping me think through this file."

"Arnie. Glad to have you aboard."

"Thanks, Bob."

"Looks like I just missed your call yesterday."

"Ted Durant came through big time."

"No question. The Sovs are up to something with the Black Sea Fleet."

"Ever seen Spetsnaz attached to them before?"

"Never. Even the boys on those ships are going to know something's up. I'll bet the rumors are flying."

"Still convinced it's Crete, Bob?"

"Unless the Greek boyfriend is a coincidence, which he isn't. Yeah, I'm convinced. Ivan's got something big planned."

"Nick thinks someone asked the boyfriend and his buddies to take a look at a couple of locs and that's about it."

"That's a good bet. Preliminary stuff from a few locals. The Sovs have moved way beyond them by now. I think we can forget about the Greek gang of four or five or whatever it was. If I was one of those boys, I'd be looking over my shoulder in case someone thinks I'm a loose end. There might be an operational cell on Crete. That would explain the drop. There are certainly plenty of tough vets from their scrape with the Nazis still on that island. We need a Greek on site. Routine stuff. Read the papers. Listen to the radio. Daily reports. Nothing heavy."

"What about our embassy?"

Arnie's suggestion makes sense. The Department of State has some of the best linguists in the American government working around the globe. But Nick's fear of escalation causes him to reject Arnie's idea.

"I'm not willing to go to State. They've got some good people there, but anything we do is going to get back to Foggy Bottom and it's just a short trip from there to the White House."

"My supply of Greeks is out. Nick?"

"I might have one we can work with."

"I'll volunteer!"

"Arnie wants to marry our spear throwing Athenian."

"As long as he survives the rehearsal dinner!"

They all laugh.

"Nick. Looks like you've got another trip to Athens. Let her know you're coming."

"She's got a job. She may not be willing to just up and leave to help out some people she barely knows."

"Use some of that cash you're always throwing around."

"Who told you about that?"

"Talk to her. She might be able to help us out, or she might be able to point us in the right direction. It's all low level stuff. No need to tell her anything other than what kind of reports you want. Leave the

Russians out of it if you can. Keep the encryption simple. If Ivan picks it up, it'll look strictly low key. If she's as smart as you think she is, she'll pick it all up in no time."

"All right. I'm going to Athens. Sorry, Arnie."

"I'll marry her on the rebound."

"In your dreams. We'll keep you posted, Bob."

"Okay. Out here."

Ben Sacolick cuts the connection as Arnie and Nick hang up. At this point there is no question in the minds of these three men: the Soviet Union is poised to make a move in the Eastern Mediterranean that could shift the world's balance of power in their favor. The last best hope for the West, short of mutually assured destruction, may rest squarely on their shoulders.

First things first, and Nick and Arnie head back downstairs to talk over how they're going to get Mika Ioannou to agree to become a CIA operative.

CHAPTER 36

PINK SLIP

Mika Ioannou's foray into the labyrinth of problems constituting the public health of Athens was exactly what she hoped for as she slogged through four years of course work at the University. When she learned that Greece's infant mortality rate–60 deaths per 1,000 live births–is nearly double the rate of Great Britain and the United States, she resolved to do what she could to change that state of affairs. Her first and only job offer after graduation was to be the lone assistant to the director of a pre- and post-natal healthcare clinic in one of the poorest neighborhoods in Athens. Perfect.

Two months after Mika's arrival, the administrator quit. Mika got a new title, no raise, and no new assistant.

Underfunded, understaffed, and under constant threat of being closed by a myopic government, the clinic is a daily lesson for Mika in the chaotic lives of the working poor in Athens. Women whose lives are a constant struggle against attitudes of the past and stunted visions of the future pour into the clinic looking for advice far beyond how to care for their soon-to-arrive or recently-arrived children. With a staff of three nurses, one part-time physician, and one custodian, Mika finds herself on any given day filling the roles of administrator, accountant, counselor, psychologist, repairman, and even health care provider. It's a crazy world, and she loves it.

Unfortunately, the government does not. As Nick Temple walks into the clinic this Monday morning, he is nearly run over by movers who are taking away the clinic's furniture, files, and anything else not nailed down, as the last drachma of public funding is due to be spent by closing time. And the Greek Parliament has made it clear that for the foreseeable future there will be no more funds. As of close of business today, Mika will be out of work, and her clients will be out of luck. But until then, the frenetic pulse of clinic business continues.

A physician motions to a seriously pregnant young woman sitting in a crowded waiting room to follow him. A nurse with a stethoscope listens to the lungs of an infant no more than a month old over the noise of the others in the waiting room: chatting mothers and grandmothers, crying infants, and moving men shouting orders to each other. Another nurse explains a pamphlet outlining what a nervous young woman, a girl of no more than 18, can expect in each of the trimesters of her pregnancy. Nick winds his way through the teaming crowd heading for what he surmises are the clinic's administrative offices in the rear past the examining rooms.

Mika looks up from her desk, sees Nick, and brushes a few stray strands of her jet black hair off her classic Greek face.

"Ah! Mr. Temple. If you're seeking pre-natal care, you're too late."

"How about post-natal care?"

Mika laughs.

"Too late for that, too."

Her dark business suit is offset by a white, cotton blouse. She is all business, but her youthful beauty is not so easily hidden. Nick, with an appreciative smile, responds.

"I'm afraid I'm misinformed. I was told this is the best clinic in Athens."

"*Was* the best clinic in Athens. The money has run out. We're closing our doors. You're lucky you didn't come by a few hours from now."

"How do you manage in this chaos?"

"Chaos? I don't notice!"

She laughs again before continuing.

"I love this work. I know I'll find some other way to help. The pendulum swings quickly in Greece. Ideas under attack one day are our cause célèbre the next. Hand me those files, will you?"

Nick turns around and sees a stack of manila folders on a file cabinet. He grabs them and hands them to Mika. She heads out of the office for the waiting room and he follows. She talks to him over her shoulder on her way to the waiting room.

"I have until three o'clock. We posted notices in the neighborhood for women to come get their files, but few have. It's not surprising. The literacy rate is not high among our clients. We don't have the people to track them all down. I go around the neighborhood after work for a week delivering as many as I can. I'll do the same for a couple hours after work today, but that's it for me."

She checks the name on a file and hands it to one of the women in the waiting room.

"Ephkharisto."

"Parakolo."

The woman leaves after thanking Mika who continues to hand out files.

She finishes, turns to Nick, and smiles.

"Now, Mr. Temple, to what do I owe the pleasure of another visit from you? If you're here to propose, the answer is 'Yes' of course. But I haven't any dowry!"

"It looks like my timing is perfect."

"Anything but. I give you two minutes more and then I have to get back to work, especially if you're not proposing."

"Not a marriage proposal, but I do have a job for you if you're interested. I'll meet you in front of the clinic after work. You're done at three?"

"We're all done at three. Meet me at my apartment at six instead. It'll give me a chance to deliver files, and then clean up for the fantastic dinner you're going to buy me."

"Six it is. I'll wear a tie."

"As you like."

Mika laughs as Nick turns and leaves. She smiles after him, wondering what the mysterious American has in mind.

CHAPTER 37

AYE, AYE

The Soviet Army's urban warfare training center in a remote corner of the Kazakh Steppe is a perfect location for the final phase of training for Captain Shevardnadze's Strike Team Two. For nearly three months he and his men have been subjected to constant drills on the Black Sea, practicing in nearly every conceivable marine condition until the team's members have collectively proven they can survive and prevail no matter what the sea might throw at them. Ultimately, their training has to shift from a successful landing and incursion to the mission itself. With a little over two months to go until the mission is live, the time is right to enter the final phase of their preparation.

Two vital aspects of their urban warfare training strike Shevardnadze as contradictory: demolition and extraction. It's a contradiction the Captain has not discussed with the men, nor will he. In the past, any demolition training Strike Team Two has undergone has been for maximum effect, maximum destruction, no survivors, no one to extract. Their current training is different. The team's focus is demolition one day, extraction the next: a day of small unit, rapid demolition deployment; technical study and implementation of plastique and detonator placement for effect on a variety of construction materials and building types; precise communication drill; and sequential radio detonation practice, followed by a day of two-man fire and maneuver teams; close quarters urban combat; and hostage rescue, extraction, and evacuation.

A mission that combines both is fraught with more than the usual risks. Timing, of course, is everything. However, either objective of the mission–hostage rescue or demolition–consumes a dangerous amount of time, making the other, if it is to be accomplished in the immediate aftermath of phase one, far less likely to succeed. It's a simple matter of opposition force response time. Shevardnadze has found himself thinking, "Pick one: rescue or demolition. But not both. That is suicide!"

The Captain is as fine a company level commander as the Soviets have to offer. He's fearless and obedient. He never considers expressing his concerns about the contradictory nature of their training either up or down the chain of command. What Shevardnadze has not considered is the simple notion that his superiors have not settled on a single course of action for the pending mission, and they want all of the Strike Teams to be at their highest level of readiness for any eventuality. They want operational flexibility, not typically a Soviet Army trait, and the Team's eclectic training agenda on the high Kazakh Steppe is a direct outgrowth of that desire.

CHAPTER 38

THE WEST COAST CHECKS IN

San Marino is a town of fine homes, manicured lawns, and swimming pools lying south and east of Cal Tech in Pasadena, California. With a little help from Dan's family, Dan and Ruthie O'Hara were able to buy a comfortable spread in San Marino when Dan went to work for the Rand Corporation in 1949. Their 1930s two-story, Mediterranean-style house sits on a generous lot that features citrus trees, a garden of flora transplanted from the east, and a pool surrounded by a sprawling patio, all recognizable signs of the good life in Southern California. The O'Haras are raising two daughters who spend most of the year in boarding schools back east. So when Ruthie's sister, Eleanor Temple, asked if she might stay with the O'Haras until she and Nick resolved their differences, Ruthie and Dan were initially delighted at the prospect of filling the house back up a bit. Ruthie in particular felt that the fresh air, sunshine, affluent friends, and Valley Hunt Club membership would all breathe new life into what Eleanor saw as her monotonous existence. As it turned out, an empty house is preferable to a morose one.

Eleanor, in spite of her upbeat reports to Nick, has done little since coming to California other than obsess over the difference between her failed marriage and her sister's stable and prosperous home life. This morning, as Eleanor Temple sits at her sister's kitchen table drinking her third cup of black coffee, she composes a letter to an old family friend at the CIA. She is threatening in less than subtle terms to expose Nick's affair with Vanessa Porter, having learned about the affair in a letter from a casual Berlin acquaintance two days ago.

Ruthie has just finished her morning swim. She comes into the kitchen wearing a terry cloth robe and drying her hair with a small hand towel. Her entrance goes unnoticed by Eleanor.

Ruthie slings her hand towel over her shoulder, grabs a highball glass out of a cabinet, and pours herself a glass of fresh-squeezed orange juice from a pitcher Dan filled before heading to work.

"Want to go for a dip? The water's great. Really clears your head first thing in the morning."

Eleanor, after a moment, looks up from her furious writing.

"Huh?"

"A swim. Want to take a swim? I'll go back in. What do you say?"

"Maybe when I'm finished here."

"Who you writing to?"

"You don't know him."

Ruthie takes a sip of her orange juice.

"Is it about Nick?"

Eleanor bursts into tears. Ruthie goes over to her sister. Eleanor desperately grabs her, hugs her, and buries her face in Ruthie's robe, sobbing and shaking. Ruthie strokes the unkempt hair on her sister's head. As Eleanor cries, Ruthie peers over her shoulder at the unfinished letter. She can't help but notice that her sister's tone has grown increasingly bitter and accusatory; she wonders when her younger sister will finally take the advice she and Dan have been giving her for months now to make a clean break and file for a divorce. The strain of having an embittered woman darken their days with no relief in sight is starting to affect her relationship with Dan. She feels something has to give, or at some point she'll be forced to choose between her sister and her husband. And Ruthie's not sure Eleanor would survive the choice that she knows she would make.

CHAPTER 39

GETAWAY DAY

Communications specialist Ben Sacolick knocks on Nick's door.

"Come in."

He cracks the door and pokes his head into Nick's office.

"Broke out another wire from Crete, Mr. Temple."

"Sure, Ben. Let's have a look."

Sacolick enters and hands the decoded communique to Nick.

"Short and sweet. Par for the course on this operation."

The report details two shipping announcements: departure time, ship's name, registry, country of origin, and tonnage, followed by the usual phrase, "Nothing more to report."

"Thanks, Ben. Did you send Ted Durant a copy?"

"Done. Is he getting anything out of them?"

"Not a thing. Standard notices. No encryption that he can see."

"Didn't think so. Not a bad gig, though. Hanging out on Crete, reading the paper for about 10 minutes, sending a quick wire."

"She's a rookie. No sense loading her up with too much. She's doing a great job for us so far. Keep me posted."

"Will do, boss."

Sacolick leaves as Nick reads the decoded report one more time.

Mika's reports from Crete are brief, precise, and so far worthless. Nick realizes that combing through six months of archived papers and two weeks of reading the local newspapers on a daily basis is hardly the sort of activity that any mission should live or die on. But if there's a clue in the local press about targets or timing, the last pieces of the puzzle they've been working on for nearly a year, then it's not going to get by him. Mika will make certain of that.

After Nick finishes reading the report he decides it's time to head down to Crete to check in with Mika and find out what he can about the Monastery near Vai. He'll meet Vanessa in Athens, and from there they'll fly together to Crete.

CHAPTER 40

BUSTED

"I don't like it, Bob."

"Hell, it's not coming from me."

"Some back channel traffic? Someone's trying to sabotage a career."

"Not strictly back channel. I've known Ellie for years. She's angry and she's trying to stick it to Nick. No question. But look, if I ignore it, she's just going to bump it up the chain. She might anyway."

What do you want from me?"

"Take a look, write a report, and that should do it."

"I don't have to take a look."

"Then write the damn report."

Arnie Miller takes a deep breath and thinks carefully about what he's going to say next.

"I'm not your man, Bob. I just can't do it. I don't even like talking about this behind Nick's back."

"All right, Arnie. I can't say as I blame you."

"You've known him forever. Why not just ask him?"

"Sure. 'Hey, Nick. Are you fucking a possible double agent even though you're still married?'"

"Why not? He's a big boy. He can take it. Besides, you're pretty sure you already know the goddamn answer."

"Okay, Arnie. I'll take care of it. Shit. If this Crete thing blows up, the last thing we need is for the front man to be sidelined because he couldn't keep it in his pants."

"You gotta do, what you gotta do."

"This isn't what I signed up for. Well, thanks at least for listening, Arnie."

Arnie Miller motions to Ben Sacolick who cuts the secure line from Berlin to D.C.

CHAPTER 41

GAME PLAN

The five men are gathered in a small, secure room at the heart of the Soviet Union's urban warfare training center. Captain Shevardnadze and his two fellow Strike Team commanders maintain an air of calm, professional detachment in spite of their collective excitement. With a map of Crete spread out before them, their company commander, Major Gregori Ulnikov, and General Colonel Fyodor Rustov, commander of the Odessa Military District, provide the first detailed briefing on the Company's mission scheduled to commence at one minute before midnight on April 30, 1955. Shevardnadze's dreams of participating in a strike of global importance are within his grasp. Years of training and months of drill have prepared him and his men for the coming moment.

The fact that their initial briefing is provided by a man as distinguished as Rustov—a hero of Stalingrad and the Battle of Berlin, a recipient of the Order of Lenin, twice decorated as a Hero of the Soviet Union—demonstrates the mission's critical importance to the highest echelons of both military and civilian leadership in the U.S.S.R.

After talking for nearly two hours about individual team responsibilities, objectives, timing, support and additional training, General Colonel Rustov turns to address the small gathering on the strategic importance of their mission.

"Comrades, your heroism will tip the balance of power in a way that commanders of entire armies can only dream of. Crete's sovereignty and alliance with the world's socialist nations will virtually ensure our domination of the Suez Canal and the world's supply of oil. We will have a base from which we can support the struggles of indigenous peoples in Africa and Central Asia. We will establish a socialist nation that reaches to the southernmost end of Europe. And we will do all of that with fewer than 200 men operating for less than 24 hours."

Shevardnadze swells with pride. Just being in the same room with someone of Rustov's stature is something he will remember for all of his days. Serving under his direct command is an unimaginable privilege. His qualms about the nature of their training are gone. His confidence in his superiors' strategic and tactical thinking is ironclad. He commands, and is commanded by, the most capable military men in all of the Soviet Union. The only unknown, the only source of any lingering doubt in his mind is the crucial element of surprise. With it, a swift victory is assured. Without it, any victory will come at the cost of horrific sacrifices. Without it, he will lead 39 men into a cauldron of fire, a living hell for which no training, drills, or exercises can possibly prepare them.

CHAPTER 42

THE COUNTDOWN BEGINS

Mika thought when she signed on with Nick that she would be caught up in a whirlwind of intrigue and action. Instead, he asked her to read a daily newspaper, Heraklion's *Patris*, and report to him all shipping notices and anything that refers to meeting times and places of government officials, especially if they are scheduled to all meet together. She started the day after she arrived by scouring the last six months of the paper's editions in the archives section of the Vikelaia Library in Heraklion. She sent Nick a meticulous report detailing each shipping notice appearing in the paper at any point during the last six months. Each day since her arrival she has read the paper's latest edition. In the last three weeks there have been plenty of stories about the Governor-General, the government-appointed administrator of Crete, and the island's four Prefects, but until today she has never come across one that refers to their all meeting together. As to the shipping notices, she cannot remember ever reading anything less interesting, less intriguing. However, true to her agreement with Nick, she notes anything she finds in her daily reports. When Nick asked her to look around for ways to get on and off Crete that might go unnoticed by the authorities, her work became slightly more interesting. Adding an idle ship's captain or a private flying service to her reports gave her a taste of the intrigue she thought she'd experience. And now, Nick and Vanessa have joined her on the island.

Vanessa's simultaneous appearance with Nick on Crete was at first a source of some disappointment. Nick's attitude towards her from the start was one of business-like detachment, an attitude she couldn't honestly remember experiencing from a man since having turned sixteen. At the University, the only men not interested in her were those not interested in women at all. She thought she might try to unwrap the enigma that is Nick Temple during their time together on this ancient and tragic island. Having met Vanessa, she now understands that her relationship with Nick will continue to be all business.

Now, instead of communicating via wire, Mika has been giving Nick daily personal briefings of what seems to her to be worthless minutiae. If the Americans did not pay so well she would have quit after the first week. But, she has to admit, spending the first half of March in Heraklion courtesy of the American taxpayers has been a welcome respite from the frenzy that was her life in Athens. And besides, she needs the job.

Today's trip to and from the east end of the island to find out what she could about a possible air drop last year was more to her taste. She found out a few things she already knew. For instance, the monks at the Toplou Monastery are a tough bunch not given to falling apart at the sight of a beautiful woman. She also found out a number of details likely of interest to Nick about a group of men from Heraklion who stayed in Palekastro for a week during the time Nick is interested in. According to the locals, every evening for four or five days in a row they would take the two Jeeps they were driving out to Vai and not come back until the next morning. After their last trip to Vai, no one Mika talked to could remember seeing them again. It took all of Mika's considerable persuasive Greek charm to extract those bits of intel out of a local innkeeper and his small circle of acquaintances.

Nick sits and drinks a late afternoon coffee as Mika, fresh back from her trip to Palekastro, reads *Patris*. The mid-March day is warm enough for the owners of the cafés on Lions Square in the heart of Heraklion to set up a smattering of outdoor tables.

"Did he say how many men there were?"

"He wasn't sure. It was a year or more ago. Four was his best guess."

"Young, old, short, tall, skinny, fat?"

"Young, skinny, and nervous."

"Niko's gang?"

"Maybe. Probably."

"Anything like a hotel register?"

Mika laughs.

"You're joking, right?"

"I knew it was a long shot. I should have gone out there months ago."

"Don't fret. You would get nothing from them. They were suspicious of an Athenian. I doubt they've talked to a foreigner since the Nazis left."

"That's why we pay you so handsomely."

Mika laughs again.

"I should demand a raise."

"Not a problem, as long as you remember who your friends are. Read that last announcement to me again."

Mika translates.

"On April 30th, the Governor-General and the Four Prefects will visit Agios Nikolaos and from there journey to the Venetian Loggia in Heraklion for . . . ."

"What time? What time are they leaving Agios Nikolaos?"

Mika continues to scan the article.

"They're spending the night, and heading to Heraklion in the morning for breakfast at the Loggia before continuing to the Prefecture."

"You're sure all five of them all spending the night in Agios Nikolaos?"

"That's what it says."

"And they'll be going to Heraklion the next morning? May Day?"

"According to the paper."

"Is this some sort of annual ritual?"

"I have no idea. I don't follow Cretan politics."

Nick slams his fist into the palm of his other hand.

"That's it then. That's why we've seen more May Day traffic than usual. There's no doubt we've got it all. Timing, targets, everything. Son of a bitch, we've got 'em! Actionable intelligence. Big time! That's the last piece. The air drop is icing on the cake. If I weren't a married man already having an affair with someone else, I'd kiss you."

Nick feels a rush of adrenaline as he contemplates the results of a year of relentless, patient intelligence work. Mika laughs at his visible excitement.

"Go to your hotel, check out, and wait for us. Vanessa and I'll get a cab and we'll all grab the night flight to Athens. We need to get the hell out of Crete."

"The second time I've been fired this month."

"Not at all. I've got another assignment for you if you're interested."

"More newspaper reading? Talking to monks? It's been a nice quiet break, but I'll pass. I'll take my chances back in Athens."

"We'll talk about it on the flight to Athens. We need you to do much more than read newspapers."

"More than reading? I'm always willing to listen. And a big fat raise, right?"

Nick laughs.

"Name your price, sweetheart!"

Mika hands Nick the newspaper.

"Okay, see you in a bit. Be careful, Mika. You're in this up to your neck now."

"Don't worry, Nick Temple. Don't you know? Greek women are immortal!"

She flashes Nick a smile, turns and walks towards her small hotel just off the square. Nick pays their tab and heads back to gather Vanessa. He knows now that time is of the essence. He needs to get to Berlin. He has less than a week to construct a detailed briefing and credible field response that he can personally deliver to Washington, D.C. He has to convince his superiors at the CIA of two vital points: First, that beginning on the night of April 30, 1955, the Soviet Union plans to initiate a swift and deadly coup d'état that, if successful, will result in the nominal independence of Crete and the creation of a major new Soviet satellite in the Mediterranean. Second, that anything beyond a surgical response aimed precisely at the imminent Soviet commando operation carries too high of a probability of resulting in nuclear conflict and, therefore, must be rejected.

CHAPTER 43

BODY COUNT

Nick reads the brief note the front desk clerk gave him. All it has is an address about four blocks from the hotel.

Nick puts the note in his pocket.

"She left nothing more?"

"She left nothing at all. The note was left by the men who took her."

"How many?"

"Three, maybe four."

"Did you call the authorities?"

"What do you mean, the authorities? They were the authorities! Who am I to stick my nose in their business? Leave or I will call the authorities at once, exactly as you wish."

Nick walks briskly to the taxi where Vanessa waits. He hands the driver a 500-drachma note.

"Wait for us."

He opens the back door of the cab and Vanessa slides out.

"I've got an address on Epimenidou, near the Customs House. I don't know what we'll find, but it's only about three or four blocks from here. We'll walk."

They take Ariadnis off the square towards the water, turning right onto Passifais and heading straight for Epimenidou. They turn left at the intersection and immediately see a small, noisy crowd gathering with more on the way. Nick and Vanessa stop at the same moment as they both lock onto the reason for the increasingly boisterous crowd. Hanging from a lamppost, the letters CIA crudely written on her white shirt with what appears to be her own blood, is the battered, lifeless body of Mika Ioannou. Two men carrying a ladder shove their way through the crowd. The high-low blare of an ambulance siren can be heard approaching.

Nick grabs Vanessa by the shoulder. They turn and retrace their steps, moving as quickly as they can to get back to the cab.

"I'm sorry you had to see that," Nick says without looking at Vanessa.

She is silent for a moment. Nick worries she is in shock, but her steady, quick pace tells him otherwise.

"I saw much worse during the war, including my husband's execution. Nothing humans do to each other has shocked me since that night."

As they turn onto the square, they can see their taxi driver, leaning against the cab, smoking. Luckily, word of Heraklion's latest murder has not traveled to this side of Lions Square. Nick whistles. The driver looks up, gets in the cab and starts the engine.

Nick opens the back door. Vanessa slides in ahead of him. As he closes the door behind him, he directs the driver.

"The airport. Quickly."

They speed away, leaving the Cold War's least deserving victim behind.

CHAPTER 44

GETTING OUT OF DODGE

From the taxi Nick can see the TAE Greek National Airlines DC-4 sitting on the tarmac. He can also see a line forming at the airport's entrance. News of Mika's murder has spread quickly over the island. A checkpoint has been set up across the only road to the airport. Armed Cretan militiamen are checking the identification of anyone trying to get to the airport. The evening flight to Athens is the only scheduled commercial flight, so even with the checkpoint, traffic is light.

Nick reaches into the bottom of his flight back, opens its false bottom, and pulls a wrapped stack of one hundred American twenty dollar bills. He leans forward to address the driver.

"Back to the harbor."

"What?"

Nick throws the money down on the seat next to the driver.

"Now! Do it!"

The driver sees the cash, executes an immediate U-turn, and heads back for the harbor in Heraklion.

Nick turns to Vanessa.

"There's a seaplane in the harbor run by a Brit ex-pat. Flies mail and other supplies to Santorini. Mika noted him in a report. He should be able to get us off the island."

The driver, who has been listening for a chance to earn more American twenty dollar bills speaks up.

"I know this man. I take you to him. Sure, I know him."

"The Venetian Harbor?"

"No. Just beyond. A small beach west of the Fortress. A pier from the beach to his plane is where he ties up. I take you."

The taxi winds its way through the tangled streets of old Heraklion heading west across town. The driver's curiosity is piqued by crowds of people gathering on the sidewalks or moving towards Lions Square. Nick sees the cabbie catching glimpses of the crowds as he drives.

Nick pulls his wallet out of his jacket breast pocket. The phone number of the ex-pat is scribbled on a scrap of paper. He looks up and sees a phone booth outside of a small shop on the next corner.

He whispers to Vanessa, "Talk to him while I make a phone call. Keep his mind on you."

"Pull up to the phone booth," he directs the driver.

Nick fishes a handful of 10 and 20 lepta coins out of his pocket and jumps out of the taxi as soon as it stops.

"Wait here. Keep the motor running."

"Sure, boss."

Nick strides to the phone booth as Vanessa waits in the taxi. At this point, Vanessa thinks to herself, their driver may be the only person in Heraklion who hasn't heard about Mika's murder. She notices that he strains to see what it is drawing the crowd. He motions to a man in the crowd to come over to the taxi.

"Is today a holiday," Vanessa asks.

"Not today."

"Why are so many people out at this hour?"

"I don't know. It's not usual for Heraklion."

"Maybe a speaker? A Communist?"

The man the driver signaled to starts across the street heading for the taxi. The driver shouts at him in Greek.

"Hey, where are you going?"

The driver turns his attention back to Vanessa.

"If it's a Communist, he'll be arrested, for sure."

"What about the crowd?"

"They'll be told to go home. Or the police will beat them."

The cabbie lights a cigarette, and before Vanessa can respond, while the man crossing the street fights his way through the traffic, Nick gets back into the cab.

"All set. Let's go."

The driver, torn between finding out why the crowd has gathered and the stack of American dollars, decides to stick with the cash. He hops in the driver's seat, puts the taxi in gear and pulls away from the curb. The man he motioned to reaches the cab as it's pulling away.

"The seaplane?" the driver asks.

"He'll meet us there. He's only two minutes away."

The driver takes one last look at the moving crowd before heading towards the west side of the Venetian fortress that separates the harbor at Heraklion from the open sea.

The Grumman G-73 Mallard's two Pratt & Whitney R-1340 radial engines are already idling when the cab pulls off the coast road and comes to a stop in a small parking lot of crushed stone that separates the road from the beach. At the north end of the lot a wooden plank footpath extends towards the water until it becomes a floating pier. Tied to the pier fifty feet out from the water's edge the Grumman awaits.

Vanessa and Nick, his flight bag in hand, get out of the cab. The driver pulls their two bags out of the trunk. A man walks towards them from the seaplane.

"Are you Temple?"

He extends his hand and Nick shakes it.

"Right. Captain White?"

"No need for that. Chalky'll do. It's what my mates called me in the war. Here, I'll take those."

Nick can't help grinning at his pilot's nickname.

"Fuckin' Brits," he thinks to himself.

Chalky White grabs the bags from the cab driver and heads towards the plane to stow them on board. Nick turns to the cabbie.

"I want you to remain here for ten minutes after we've left. There are two thousand American dollars in that stack I gave you, and I expect that should be enough to buy ten more minutes of your time."

"Sure, boss. Ten minutes. No problem."

Chalky White returns.

"Now, about the fare."

Nick pulls him aside.

"Can we do that once we're aboard?"

"I've no objection. But it's got to be before we're airborne. You understand, of course. Business is business."

"Of course."

"All right. Here we go, then. Stay to the center. Don't want anyone going for a swim, what?"

Nick and Vanessa follow Chalky down the middle of the pier to the aircraft. A local assistant stands ready to cast off. White stops short of the prop. Nick and Vanessa board through the cabin door directly beneath the overhead wing. Nick looks back quickly to make sure the taxi driver hasn't left. He hasn't. He's leaning against the cab smoking a cigarette and checking his watch.

Once inside the seaplane, Nick and Vanessa take two of the main cabin's six seats. White pops his head in.

"All settled then?"

"We're fine, thank you."

"You said Brindisi over the blower."

"Is that a problem?"

"None. Brindisi it is. Five thousand American should do it."

"I thought we were allies."

White lets out a hearty laugh.

"I say, Temple. Right you are. Wouldn't do it for anyone but the Yanks. And that's the truth, what?"

Nick reaches into his flight bag, pulls out three stacks of one hundred twenty dollar bills and hands them to White.

"There's six grand. After you drop us off at Brindisi I want you to fly to Palermo, land, refuel, and then return to Heraklion. And I want your flight log to record a round trip, Heraklion to Palermo and back."

"Palermo is lovely this time of year, especially with a few American dollars in one's pocket. Consider it done. The subterfuge a pen affords one is simply spectacular, what?"

White climbs into the cockpit and shuts the cockpit's narrow, oval wooden door behind him. His assistant closes the cabin door from the outside. Nick and Vanessa settle in as the seaplane quickly pulls away from the dock. White opens the throttle; the seaplane accelerates, and eventually skips just over the bay's surface before going into a slow climb heading for the small town of Brindisi about half-way up the heel of Italy's boot.

"I'll contact our man in Naples when we land. He'll be able to get us to Berlin."

"Nothing like a suitcase full of cash to move things along," Vanessa observes.

"Beats trying to shoot our way out."

Vanessa reaches across the aisle and takes Nick's hand.

"A night in Brindisi?" she asks.

"We'll have to."

"I'm not disappointed."

Nick looks at Vanessa. He flashes back to their first meeting at the Wannsee Chateau when she as much as told him she wanted in on the high-stakes game he plays every day. He let her in, and for better or for worse her personal safety is now his responsibility. The hell of it is that his years of training and service tell him that no one person is more valuable than the mission. So he focuses instead on what lies ahead:

Berlin, Washington, D.C., and if all goes well, back to Crete for the most important mission of his life.

CHAPTER 45

TEA FOR TWO

Vanessa Porter looks forward to her time on the Wannsee with Nick tomorrow. She hasn't seen him since their hasty return from Crete via Brindisi and Naples. She knew he'd be working night and day to get ready for D.C., so a day of sailing before they head out of Berlin again will be a welcome break for them both. When she received Malenkov's message, she decided to handle it on her own; she decided that involving Nick would interrupt the far more important task of his prepping for D.C.

She gets out of the taxi on the north side of the traffic circle around the Siegessäule, the famed Victory Tower, in Berlin's Tiergarten. After paying her fare she walks to the Tiergarten's newest addition, the recently opened English Garden Teahouse. The late March weather is surprisingly mild for Berlin. As comfortable as Vanessa is, her experience tells her that the weather won't last.

The Tiergarten is just starting to recover from being denuded for firewood during and immediately after World War II. Thanks to the efforts of people from all over Europe, the vast park in the city's heart that Vanessa remembers so fondly from the years before the war has been largely replanted and is starting to look like a park again rather than a barren and depressing reminder of the war's deprivations.

Today Vanessa hardly notices the recent changes. Her imminent meeting with Vasily Malenkov, the first since last year at the end of May, has her full attention. As she approaches, she sees Malenkov waiting for her on a bench. As always, he is dressed in a manner more suited to an English gentleman on his way to his London club–highly polished black oxfords, three-piece, pin-striped suit, light overcoat unbuttoned to take advantage of the temperate climate–than the coldblooded KGB operative that he is. She walks up to him.

"Are we going inside?"

"No need for that. This isn't a social visit, Vanessa."

She sits down next to him.

"Then what is it, Vasily?"

Vanessa's question is matter of fact, almost stern.

"Can we at least be civil? How have you been?"

"I'm certain that you could tell me how I've been."

"Paranoia? Not a flattering trait, my dear."

"Realism. You forget, Vasily. I've been through worse. Now, please tell me why you've summoned me here."

"Summoned? Ha! You overestimate my power."

Vanessa stands up.

"I'm not interested in subtle banter, Vasily. It is over between us, and I don't care to spend any more time in your company."

Malenkov stands up facing her and no more than twelve inches away. He puts his hands on her upper arms, squeezes tightly, and in a low, malevolent tone asks, "How did you enjoy Crete?"

A look of horror flashes across Vanessa's face.

"Be thankful it wasn't you hanging from that lamppost, Frau Porter. Your friendship with Mr. Temple is an insult."

Vanessa recovers in time to respond.

"It's an awful business you two are in."

"This isn't business. It's personal."

"Then it was a clumsy personal message. Why not just write a letter instead of killing such a beautiful young woman?"

"Perhaps next time I will."

"There isn't going to be a next time, Vasily. We've been through for months. Now unless you plan to shoot me right here, I will be on my way."

Malenkov's grip on Vanessa's upper arms tightens to the point of causing pain for just an instant. Her face reveals nothing, so he releases her arms and steps back as a strained smile crosses his lips.

"As you wish, of course."

Vanessa developed the inner strength to maintain her outer composure during five years of Nazi threats, suspicion, surveillance, and interrogation. She calls on every ounce of that strength as she turns to walk back towards the Victory Tower well aware that at any moment a single 9mm round from Vasily's Makarov PM could end her tragic life.

CHAPTER 46

TACKING TO WINDWARD

The cool breeze is a manageable 7 – 12 knots out of the southwest, more than enough air to move around the lively 5.5 meter Flying Dutchman with Nick Temple at the tiller. The boat runs easily downwind, its jib and main set wing on wing as Nick keeps a close eye on the trim of each.

He and Vanessa have not exchanged a word since she told him shortly after getting underway that she met with Vasily Malenkov in the Tiergarten yesterday. Nick is sorting through his reactions, personal and professional, as he falls off just enough to port to bring the jib onto the same tack as the main. They continue effortlessly downwind with Nick sitting to starboard in the stern sheets, and Vanessa slightly forward to port.

"If you decide to meet with Malenkov again, will you let me know in advance?"

Without looking back at Nick, Vanessa responds.

"I will. It was his idea."

"Either way, you'll let me know, right? It's too dangerous at this point to do these things alone."

"For me?"

"Of course."

"It's more than that though, isn't it?"

"Yes, it's more than that. But that's where it starts."

"Does it worry you?"

"That's my job. You're as capable as anyone I've ever met in this business, but there's no reason to go it alone. There's simply too much at stake now. And that includes your life."

Nick feels the breeze shift slightly. He nudges the bow to starboard to keep the wind off his quarter.

"And if you didn't have to worry about me?"

"It's too late for that."

"I can disappear. I've done it before."

She's giving Nick a way out, one he doesn't want and rejects instantly.

"Closer is better, for many reasons." Some of those reasons are purely selfish, Nick acknowledges to himself.

They sail downwind for another ten minutes in silence before Nick speaks up.

"What did he want?"

"To frighten me."

"He's a sadist."

"I told him we're all in an awful business when a beautiful young woman like Mika is so casually sacrificed."

"Did the son of a bitch laugh?"

"No. But he said it wasn't business; it was personal, that I was lucky it wasn't me hanging from the lamppost."

"Then he hasn't put it together."

"What?"

"His ego is getting in the way. He's a vindictive, murderous prick, and that's working in our favor."

"Is it? Mika would disagree."

"His relationship with you is still clouding his judgment almost a year after it ended. That doesn't surprise me."

"An obsession?"

"Maybe." He pauses. "Or maybe just a sick bastard with time on his hands. I think we'd have seen more from him over these last ten months if you were an obsession for him. If killing Mika was personal, then he has no idea what he told you when he was drunk, or that we've got a lock on Mother Russia's next move. He hasn't put it together. Mika was a personal message."

"That's precisely how I phrased it."

"What was his reaction to that?"

"I thought he was going to kill me on the spot."

"But he didn't. If it was business, he would have. At the most he wouldn't have let you live through the night. He doesn't have a clue."

Nick checks the wind.

"You're leaving Berlin with me tomorrow."

"I'm not going to Washington."

"Not Washington, Paris. Just for a week while I'm in D.C."

"And what am I to do in Paris for week?"

"Stay alive. Your chances are better there than here."

Vanessa doesn't argue with the prospect of putting some distance between herself and the brutality of Vasily Malenkov.

"We're getting too far downwind of the Club. It's going to take us the rest of the day beating to windward to get back. We'd better start."

With that, Nick puts the tiller over to port until the wind is on his beam. Slowly, steadily he hauls in both main and jib as he brings the bow as close to the wind as he can without luffing. Vanessa joins Nick to starboard for ballast as the boat heels to leeward. The gentle motion of flying downwind is replaced by the boat's steady pounding on the lake's small waves as they work against the prevailing breeze.

CHAPTER 47

PRE-FLIGHT JITTERS

The Pan American World Airways Douglas DC-6B waits on the tarmac at Tempelhof. Passengers for the morning flight to Paris include Nick Temple and Vanessa Porter. They gather inside the spacious terminal's main waiting area as boarding is imminent. Nick wears a navy blue business suit and a light overcoat. Vanessa's jacket and dress paint the picture of a successful European businessman's wife going on a brief holiday abroad – formal without being showy, relaxed without being casual.

"I'll pick you up in Paris on my way back from D.C."

"We've been over it. You should try to relax."

"I can't. We're getting too close."

"You and I?" Vanessa teases.

"No. I mean to the operation."

"Maybe D.C. will take over."

Arnie Miller stands off to the left by a bank of payphones keeping watch. Nick checks his watch against the large clock at the far end of the terminal.

"That would give us spring in Paris."

"It sounds lovely."

"I wouldn't count on it."

A voice comes over the terminal intercom announcing boarding for flight 1242, Pan American World Airways non-stop to Paris.

"You should have checked that bag."

"Force of habit. I always keep my flight bag with me. My portable bank."

"Enough for an overnight in Paris?"

"Who told you?"

"I'm getting better at your own game."

"I know. It's scary."

"Nick, do you think we should?"

"I can't think of any good reason why we shouldn't. Brindisi and the long winter nights settled that for me."

"And for me."

They stand. Nick grabs his black leather flight bag and looks over at Miller who signals all clear. Vanessa holds the inside of Nick's upper arm as they head out to the tarmac where their aircraft awaits, its door open, a portable stairway fast against it. The late Berlin morning is clear with a slight breeze out of the west, a perfect day for flying. The forecast is for the fine weather to soon give way to a storm off the Baltic to the north.

CHAPTER 48

THE LAYOVER

The DC-6B takes just under two hours gate to gate to fly from Berlin to Paris. As the flight touches down at Paris-Orly airport, Nick Temple and Vanessa Porter are deep in thought about the next 24 hours. Nick's decision to stay the night carries emotional and security risks that blend together in a way that few couples have to contemplate.

"Our reservation is under the name of Mr. and Mrs. Taft. Harry Taft's an old friend who works out of Prague these days. Here's your passport."

Nick hands Vanessa a forged passport complete with recent travel stamps that indicate she has been touring Europe for a number of weeks.

"No disrespect meant to your late husband."

"Of course not. I understand."

She leafs through the stamped pages of the passport.

"I've never actually been to Barcelona. I hope there isn't a test."

The aircraft comes to a halt on the tarmac. Vanessa leans over and Nick reflexively kisses her. She has mixed feelings about the coming week's arrangements. Understanding that the French might not have been predisposed to welcome the widow of a German Army officer, she has not been to the city since before the war and looks forward to reacquainting herself with Paris. She also realizes that this is not simply a romantic holiday, but a ruse for her personal safety as she dives deeper into the most dangerous geopolitical struggle of the day. For a woman who has spent many years relying on her own wits, the feeling that for the time being she has to rely on Nick and a small group of his countrymen to make certain crucial decisions is unsettling.

After consulting at length with his fellow agents, Nick selected the small Hôtel du Brésil, situated in the Latin Quarter at 10 rue Le Goff, for their one night stay and Vanessa's week alone. A block from the Jardin du Luxembourg, and near the Pantheon and other Left Bank landmarks, the hotel's location is charming, convenient, and discreet. Nick spent a month in Paris, much of it in the Latin Quarter, immediately after it was liberated in August of 1944 as a reward for a particularly successful sabotage mission deep behind German lines. His personal familiarity with the area around the Boulevards Saint-Michel and Saint-Germain was an important factor in selecting the hotel. The fact that two of the Company's men in Paris live and work within a block of the hotel helped seal the deal.

Check-in goes without a hitch. No test about Barcelona; no awkward questions; just a polite clerk working the small reception desk of an unassuming hotel on La Rive Gauche.

Once in their room, Nick exchanges his suit for a sweater and slacks. Vanessa replaces her heels with flats and sits on the bed.

"I should like to get a drink and something to eat. Then, perhaps, we could take a stroll in the park?"

"The Café de Cluny is nearby. From there we can walk easily to the Jardin du Luxembourg," Nick offers.

"That sounds lovely."

Vanessa offers her hand to Nick, and hand in hand they leave the hotel.

A light alfresco lunch washed down with a crisp 1953 Pouilly-Fuissé, followed by a slow stroll along the crushed-stone paths of the Jardin du Luxembourg are all prelude to a late afternoon in their modest hotel room. For a few hours they forget about spies of all stripes, security threats, the Cold War, Berlin, Crete, Moscow, Washington, and the rest of their lives. Instead, for a few hours they deeply feel the transcendent experience of spring in Paris.

CHAPTER 49

WELCOME HOME

Nick Temple unpacks his bag in his room at the Statler Hotel, his usual digs when he comes to D.C. The transatlantic flight gave him time to fine tune what he knows will be the most important briefing of his professional career. It also gave him time to try to compartmentalize the most important 24 hours of his personal life since the birth of his son. The process of compartmentalization, while important, is necessarily incomplete. For better or worse, Nick's plan for thwarting the Soviet Union's daring escalation of the Cold War contemplates a role for Vanessa. Somehow he has to muster the emotional detachment necessary to ask her to put herself in harm's way. He knows she'll agree to whatever he asks of her. And that means he may have to face having to complete the mission knowing the harm he fears has come to pass. Although he's convinced that taking the mission out of his hands and turning the entire matter over to the President and his cabinet would be a potentially disastrous strategic error, part of him can't help hoping for just such an outcome.

He is about to grab the mission file out of his briefcase when the room phone rings.

"Hello."

"I have a Mr. Bob Arnold on the line for you, sir."

"Okay, operator. Put him through."

"Nick, Bob Arnold. Glad to see you made it safely."

"Bob, thanks for calling. We get an audience?"

"You bet. The briefing's on for 1400 hours tomorrow. Why don't you come by first thing in the a.m. to work on the presentation?"

"Done. Your office at six thirty?"

"I'll be here. Nick, there's one other thing."

"Shoot."

"Ellie called. She wanted to know if you're in town."

"When was this?"

"About ten minutes ago."

"No sweat, Bob. My guess is she'll call here next. She knows my habits, good and bad."

"Okay. I just thought you should know."

"Sure thing, Bob. Thanks, and I'll see you in the morning."

"I'll be here."

"Have a pot of coffee ready."

"Done."

Nick hangs up. He doesn't even have time to think about how the next phone call might go when the phone rings again. It's the hotel's switchboard operator again.

"Mrs. Temple calling for you long distance, sir."

"Thank you, operator. Please put her through."

"Nick?"

"Ellie. Bob Arnold said you might call."

"Don't blame him. I put him on the spot when I asked him if you were in town."

"Of course not. How are you?"

"The kids say they miss you."

"Nicely put."

"What?"

"Skip it. How about you?"

"I'd be better if my husband wasn't having an affair. I did make a few friends in the seven years I spent raising your children, cooking your meals, and cleaning your house in Berlin. One of them was kind enough to let me know what she and probably everyone else in Berlin saw."

Nick, unsure how to respond, doesn't.

"Are you still there?"

"Yes, Ellie."

"Well?"

"Look, our marriage has been over for some time. Let's be honest."

"That's not what the paperwork says. I started to write you a letter, but I tore it up. Damn it, Nick. How could you?"

"I'm not going to go into it over the phone. But what did you expect? We've been living apart since last summer. Hell, we hardly even write each other anymore. Does that sound like a marriage?"

"Call me old fashioned, but until a judge says we're not married, I expected you to behave. God knows I have, and it hasn't been easy."

"I don't expect it has. You should file, or would you prefer I get things going?"

Ellie bursts into tears at the mention of divorce. She grew up with her parents' nearly idealized version of marriage as her model. Add to that the fact that by all appearances her older sister has settled into as comfortable a marriage as one can imagine. To be the first one in her family whose marriage is a public disaster is almost more than she can take. Nick waits for her to get ahold of herself as he wonders how she found out about Vanessa. Then he remembers the brief encounter at dinner before La Traviata.

"You'll be hearing from my lawyer," is all Eleanor Temple can muster before slamming the receiver down.

Nick slowly hangs up the phone. He walks into the bathroom, leans over the sink, and splashes some cold water on his face. He straightens up, dries his face, and looks at himself in the mirror for a moment.

"Shit. Great timing, Nick," he thinks to himself.

He splashes some more cold water on his face, dries off, and hangs up the hand towel. He returns to his bedroom, pulls a TOP SECRET file out of his flight bag, sits down in the room's one chair, and gets back to work. Nick Temple's personal problems, and there are a pile of them at the moment, are going to have to wait.

CHAPTER 50

THE PITCH

With Bob Arnold on the team, Nick is confident the briefing will produce the results they both want. The Director is about to hear from two of the most respected voices in the Company. They're in synch on the analysis and what the country's next move should be. Nick knows he's living on borrowed time, that if the Director gets a clear picture of his relationship with Vanessa, if he knows that Nick is playing slap and tickle with a Wehrmacht widow of reasonably questionable allegiance, that he'll be on the shortest of leashes. With less than four weeks to go until all hell breaks loose, Nick's value to the operation should be high enough to insulate him from any sanction at least until the mission is complete. He's counting on it. Of course, if the whole thing goes south, they'll all be on the streets and his relationship with Vanessa won't really matter a whole hell of a lot.

Cornell Bailey's a wild card. The Special Assistant to the Director has a well-deserved reputation for having no qualms about exposing others if he thinks it will further his own career. If Bailey gets wind of the link between Nick and Vanessa, there's no telling what might happen to the operation. It's going to be tough enough to sell and execute without having to put up with some rear echelon static from the likes of Bailey.

As Nick enters the briefing room just behind Bob Arnold he clears his mind to focus on the task at hand – solid analysis presented clearly and concisely, followed by an aggressive operational posture that has the feel of the only plausible alternative. He and Arnold decided to go with the shock value of the Soviet plan to open the meeting. Might as well come out punching.

The Director is already seated in his customary spot–next to the only phone in the small amphitheater–with Cornell Bailey two seats to his left. Arnold and Temple agreed that Nick would make the presentation. Arnold doesn't suffer fools gladly and would likely say something they might both regret if Cornell Bailey decides to get in the mix.

Arnold takes a seat in the back next to the projection room door and lights a cigar. He knows the cigar will annoy the Special Assistant, but, as he said to Nick in the hall, he doesn't give a shit. Walt, the projection room operator, stands at the ready. Nick strides to the podium on the far left side of the small stage in the front of the room. He places a TOP SECRET file on the podium, opens it, and looks up to the projection room.

"May I proceed, sir?"

"No one else is coming so fire away, Nick."

"Thank you, sir. Walt?"

The lights in the amphitheater dim, and a full-color image of a small, Mediterranean town appears on the screen to Nick's left. The image is so serene, so devoid of any hint of intrigue or crisis, that it could easily be a travel agency poster.

"Gentlemen, you're looking at the town of Agios Nikolaos. This small town on the north side of Crete sits square in the crosshairs of the Soviet Union's Black Sea Fleet. An attack that can be traced directly to the ambitions of Premier Nikita Krushchev is planned for the night of April 30th. The centerpiece of the attack will be five political assassinations in Agios Nikolaos designed to create a leadership vacuum on Crete into which members of the KKE, the Greek Communist Party, will step. They will declare Crete to be an independent state, and that declaration will be immediately recognized by the Soviet Union and her allies. When the smoke clears, Crete will become another captive satellite of the Soviet Union, giving Krushchev a de facto naval fortress in the Eastern Mediterranean from which the Soviet Union can control the Dardanelles, the Sea of Marmara, the Bosphorus, the Aegean and Libyan Seas, and, eventually the Suez Canal."

Temple's claim is so audacious that the Director needs a moment to collect his thoughts. If Arnold and Temple are right, there is every likelihood that an all-out nuclear war fought with the recently-deployed hydrogen bomb is a month away. Cornell Bailey sees the pause as an opportunity to go on the offensive; he is the first to react.

"The two of you have alerted Defense and State, I take it."

"No, sir, we have not. Our judgment is that such an alert will lead to a confrontation that will with a high degree of certainty result in a war, likely a nuclear war fought with hydrogen bombs, between the United States and the Soviet Union."

"Well, that's not your call. You know damn well that if you have actionable intelligence of this magnitude the full resources of the American government have to be brought to bear."

Bailey's bluster is irritating. Bob Arnold is about to respond when the Director intervenes.

"April 30th? Are you certain?"

Rather than give Bailey a tongue lashing, Bob Arnold decides it's time to bring his considerable reputation to the team's defense.

"Yes, sir. Our analysis says Saturday, April 30th. It's a lock. The assassinations will take place Saturday night, and the new government will be installed the next morning, May Day. The timing, if you gentlemen disagree with our approach, gives both Defense and State enough lead time to decide on a coordinated response that differs or supports our proposed operational posture."

An awkward silence follows as the Director digests the enormity of what two rock-solid Company men with no history of anything other than cool-headed expertise followed by decisive, focused action, have just relayed. Nick decides to add an historic note that should resonate with his bosses.

"In essence, the Sovs have stolen a page out of our own playbook."

Bailey immediately puffs up to dispute any correlation between the activities of the despised Reds and his own country.

"Just how do you figure, Temple?" he sneers.

Addressing Nick by his last name is a mistake. It makes Bailey look likes he's on a different team. Before Nick can answer, the Director breaks in.

"Panama in 1903. Their revolution was really our revolution. Warship in the harbor, a few key arrests, isolate important military assets, and before you know it, a new country signing a cozy treaty with Uncle Sam."

Bob Arnold bursts into laughter.

"Damn right, Mr. Director. Just the way we figure it. If I'm Ivan I'm thinking, 'It worked once. Let's see if it'll work again. And this time it'll be someone shoving it to the Yanks for a change.' And there are enough Cretans who want out from under Greece, and enough persecuted Communists from their Civil War and the last five years, that it just might work."

Bailey, embarrassed by his failure to see the historic analog, glowers at Arnold who puffs away on his cigar. The Director steps in to repair the damage done to his Special Assistant's ego.

"Cornell's correct, of course. If the two of you are right about what Nick just ran through, it should have been on my radar a long time ago."

"With all due respect, sir, the final pieces, particularly the dates and the hard targets for carrying out the executions, didn't fall into place until about a week ago. If we'd come to you earlier, the level of guesswork would have been too high to justify committing any assets, let alone the Defense and State Departments, to a response."

"Why not let the Soviets know?"

Bailey's question is stunningly reasonable. If the Soviets know they may be walking into an ambush, perhaps they'll call the entire operation off. But letting your enemy know you have their plans also violates a cardinal rule of intelligence work. If your enemy knows what you know, he can figure out *how* you came to know it. And *how* intelligence is gathered is often far more important than the information itself.

"What about it, Nick? If we can avoid the bloodshed and a possible Soviet takeover of the Eastern Med with a phone call, maybe we should do it."

The Director is intrigued by Bailey's suggestion.

"I'll leave that decision to you policy makers. Whether phone calls, negotiations, or even a shot across the Soviet Union's bow can forestall the attack is a decision that's well above my pay grade. What I do know is that the likelihood of an imminent attack is high, nearly a certainty, and we have a limited amount of time within which to mount an effective field response, should the powers that be decide that one is required."

"Why not let the Greeks handle it? Or just write the check with the Greeks at the laboring oar?" Bailey suggests.

"There's no doubt the Greeks are a tough lot, especially the Cretans. The Nazis found that out in a hurry. Of course, our concern is if they don't handle it. The prospect of breaking away from Greece may be too attractive, even if it's on terms dictated by the Russians. Once the Russians are in, prying them out is a whole different ballgame."

Nick waits to see if his credibility is strong enough to allow him to continue, or if the Director is going to pick up the phone and call in the big boys.

The Director stares at the phone for a minute. On one level, he'd like to dish the entire matter. He's in a tight spot, and he knows it. But he didn't rise to the head of the most powerful intelligence agency in the free world by dodging tough assignments. He looks up at Nick, pointing a finger at him as if lecturing him.

"All right. You've got about 15 minutes to convince me how you got here and why the hell I shouldn't fire the both of you right before I pick up this phone and call the Secretary of Defense, the Secretary of State, or the Soviet Ambassador."

"Fair enough," Nick responds.

"Next slide, Walt."

The image on the screen changes to a passport picture of Nikos Lendaris.

Nick continues the briefing.

"The almost comical death of this young man is where the trail began a year ago."

CHAPTER 51

GREEN LIGHT

As Nick Temple and Bob Arnold walk down the hall towards the Director's office, they discuss what the last minute summons might entail. Nick was in Arnold's office about to leave for a hop out of Andrews when the Director's secretary phoned to say they were expected in his office in five minutes. Having heard nothing from the Director subsequent to the briefing led Nick to believe he'd screwed up big time, that the matter was now being placed into the hands of actors well-beyond his small circle.

"Maybe we'll both be on the street before the day's over," Arnold offers.

"Can I use you for a reference?" Nick asks.

"Hell no! You're the guy that got me fired."

"We can open our own shop."

"Fuck that, I've got an Army pension. I've got my eye on a sweet fishing village down on the Yucatan. You're on your own, son."

They both smile as they turn into the outer office area where the Director's secretary sits.

"He told me to send you in as soon as you got here."

They comply. Nick knocks on the door and without waiting for an answer opens it.

Not surprisingly, the Director of Central Intelligence, the chief intelligence officer of the most powerful country in the world, has an office that is luxurious by anyone's standards in 1955. It has the feel of the office of a president of an Ivy League university.

Nick sits in a stuffed chair opposite the Director who is behind his enormous walnut desk. Bob Arnold picks out a seat on the leather couch against the far wall. Cornell Bailey, who is already on the couch, neither stands to greet Arnold nor acknowledges him in any other way. The cold rainy day is offset by the fire burning in the fireplace at the opposite end of the room. Two high-back chairs in front of the fireplace face the center of the room. Agents Bill Johnson and Kyle Richardson occupy the two chairs. The room's deep cherry paneling hides two doors: one to the Director's private bathroom, and the other to a small room for those so inclined to listen in on the Director's conversations without being detected. They are invariably doing so at the Director's orders.

"Nick, Bob, thanks for being available."

They both nod.

"I had a talk with the President late this afternoon."

Nick squirms slightly in his chair. He is certain that the entire matter is now about to be bumped up to the big shots at State and Defense. He's already formulating his Parisian vacation plans with Vanessa when the Director continues.

"You men should give him more credit. He's a quick study, asked all the right questions, and bought the entire package. He agrees that if Defense gets ahold of this thing it'll blow up into a crisis that none of us might easily survive"

Nick realizes he's better at reading what's on the mind of the Soviet Union's leaders than he is at reading what's on the mind of his own president. He glances over at the plump Cornell Bailey who can barely contain his disappointment.

"It didn't take much to convince him to go with the only plan we've got at the moment. So, congratulations. Everyone who matters agrees that the fate of the West's influence in the Eastern Mediterranean is squarely on your shoulders. In other words, no pressure, just don't screw up."

The six men laugh, some more nervously than others.

"Nick, you're sure you're up to this, right?"

"No doubt about it, sir. I can't guarantee it's going to work, but I think it's our best shot."

"Agreed. Bob, you know Kyle and Bill."

Bob nods to the two seated men.

"And Nick, I believe you know Bill."

"I do, indeed."

"Kyle's a Korean War vet, a 1st Recon Marine, and great in a firefight."

Richardson nods to Nick.

"I've attached them to your team. They're good men and given the scope of your plan, I'm sure you can use them."

Nick, grateful for the skilled assistance of a couple of Company men, lets the Director know.

"Thank you, sir. You're absolutely right." Nick turns to the two men. "Glad to have you on board, gentlemen. Ted Durant, over at NSA, is going to give us a hand, too."

"I know Ted. That's a good pick. I also talked the President into ordering the attachment of 10 men from the 10th Special Forces Group in Bad Tölz that you requested in your briefing. They'll go TDY to Berlin Brigade and they'll be billeted there. Contact the Brigade Deputy Commander when you get back to Berlin. I think that takes care of the additional manpower needs divided between the hotel and the radio station, outlined in your operations brief."

"It does. We'll be outnumbered, but they won't be expecting any organized resistance. That's our advantage."

"There is one big fat caveat to all of this, of course."

"Sir?"

"This plan of yours had better work, or a lynch mob will string us all up thirty minutes after the Soviets announce they've stolen Crete from us. This President does not want to go down in history as the President who lost Crete and the Eastern Med. Got it?"

"That's not going to happen, sir."

"I hope you're right, Nick. I hope you're right."

The Director stands up to signal the meeting's end. The others stand as well.

"Good luck, gentlemen. Nick, since you're heading up this effort, I want thorough and consistent situation reports from you. If you can set up comms on Crete without giving the show away, do it. I'll have authorizations drawn up for your materiel and transportation needs outlined in your briefing. Take the hop out of Andrews at 2300. The paperwork will be on board, and you can get what you need from Berlin Brigade or 7th Army HQ in Stuttgart. Good luck, gentlemen."

They all stand up. Nick and Bob shake hands with the Director before leaving. Cornell Bailey stays behind. As soon as Nick and the others are in the hallway, Nick speaks up.

"I suggest we all meet in Bob's office. I hope you guys are already packed. The hop leaves in five hours, and we need that time to work."

"Let's get to it," is Bill Johnson's response.

"The sooner the better," comes from Kyle Richardson.

"Fine. Then let's get to work. Kyle, tell me a little about yourself while we walk."

The men head as a group to Bob Arnold's office.

"Not much to tell, sir. Joined the Corps right out of college when the Korean War broke out. 1st Recon for the duration. Joined the Company when I mustered out."

"Languages?"

"Russian in college. Picked up some German since coming on board, sir."

"Married?"

"No, sir."

"Perfect. And, Kyle?"

"What's that, sir?"

"It's Nick, not sir."

"Got it, Nick."

The four men, already anonymous Cold War heroes, are about to set into motion what is not the largest, but perhaps the most daring response to Soviet aggression in the early history of the CIA.

CHAPTER 52

THE HARD WORK BEGINS

Bob Arnold's office is crowded and filled with cigar smoke. None of the four men seem to notice. These are all men who have spent nights crouching in frozen foxholes, days standing and walking in mud, weeks covered in bugs, and months eating C-rations, K-rations, or anything they could scrounge from the locals – French, Italians, Moroccans, Germans, Turks, and Koreans to name a few. A few hours in a stuffy office doesn't even register as an inconvenience.

They're poring over a detailed map of Crete. It's large enough to include the streets of Agios Nikolaus, Heraklion, Souda, and Mournies. Their attention is focused on the location of a rustic, ten-room hotel in Agios Nikolaos, one of only two hotels in the entire town.

"We need to secure those hotel rooms before the Governor-General and the Prefects arrive."

Kyle Richardson speaks up for the first time.

"Bill's right. We need someone inside that hotel. A quiet tourist, but someone who can command the staff's attention, a diversion."

"I agree, and I have someone in mind for the job. Let's step back for a minute to take a look at what we'll be facing."

They all nod, agreeing to turn the floor over to Nick.

"The Spetsnaz Company, as confirmed by the Sinop intercept, has 120 commandos assigned to it. But these are the Soviets, and there is no way they're going to throw the whole unit into the mix on the initial thrust; they're going to hold at least one-third of their force, 40 men, an entire Strike Team in reserve. It's standard doctrine for them, and I don't see them deviating on this mission."

"Besides the doctrine, it makes good tactical sense: small beaches, narrow streets in the towns, and narrow roads between towns all point to a smaller, not larger force," Bob Arnold offers.

"Bob's right. Doctrine aside, too many men in these tight spaces puts the mission at risk. That leaves a max of a forty-man team at each loc."

"Out of the forty, they've got to keep some on the beach to protect their withdrawal and their rear flank," Kyle Richardson observes.

"The kid's right, Nick."

"No doubt about it. At least two for each craft on the beach. Four craft per Strike Team. That's at least eight men on the beach to guard their withdrawal or, if needed, retreat. That leaves 32 per Strike Team on each mission."

"The numbers are still rough. What are we looking at?"

"The men from Bad Tölz bring us up to somewhere around 15 or 16."

"Four to one. Wow." Bill Johnson shakes his head at the prospect of being badly outnumbered.

Nick tries to relieve some of Bill's understandable anxiety.

"But we know they're coming, and they have no idea we'll be there. They're thinking a few Crete municipal policemen they can roll right over or even bribe into instant allegiance. The way I figure it, if they had the element of surprise, there's no way the Greeks would be able to mount a timely and effective response. That'll be Ivan's mindset going in. But we're going to hit them once they've finished their deployment. They'll be as thin at that moment as any during the night. We'll take out the rear echelon on the beach with a sniper at each location. Their men will be spread out and exposed. It'll be like shooting fish in a barrel. If they leave a comms man on the beach, we'll take him out first. The operational units will hear the gunfire, but they'll have no idea what's going on."

"What about the inflatables?"

Kyle's question is a good one. If the inflatables are destroyed, the remaining Strike Team members are going to be forced to shoot it out, maybe until they're all dead. If the inflatables are left intact, the teams may just load them up and get the hell out of there to limit the damage. Nick and Bob settled on the second option some days ago.

"We're not going to touch them. We want to kill the mission, and if they break off and head back for the open water, we'll let them do it. No sense trapping them and getting into a prolonged firefight."

"Besides the beach, how do you propose to deploy the rest of this enormous force we've assembled?"

Bob Arnold handles Bill Johnson's question.

"Hell, Bill, there's nothing to it. I mean, we're going to have at least five men in each town. The Commies haven't got a chance!"

They all laugh.

Nick checks his watch.

"We need to get out to Andrews to catch that 2300 hop."

With that announcement, the mood changes back to all business. The men begin to roll up the maps they've been using and place the TOP

SECRET files containing every scrap of information they've acquired about the mission, detailed analyses of the enemy's anticipated actions, and their still-evolving operational response, into their flight bags.

Bob Arnold speaks up.

"Call when you get to Berlin. I'll keep an eye on this end for you. Good luck, gentlemen."

They all shake hands with Bob. Nick can't help thinking that he should ask Bob to come along for the ride. But he decides to give the man whose been serving his country every day of his life since 1933 a break.

Nick Temple, Bill Johnson, and Kyle Richardson walk out of Bob Arnold's office. Whether the world is about to witness a failed Cold War coup or the beginning of the end is in the hands of these men.

CHAPTER 53

MUSCLING UP

The "war room" on the top floor of Nick's Zehlendorf office has never been this full. Nick, Ted Durant, Kyle Richardson, Bill Johnson, and ten men from the 10th Special Forces Group out of Bad Tölz crowd around a table covered with maps, files, diagrams, schedules, charts, and a variety of other documents critical to the upcoming mission. The map of Berlin that normally covers one wall has been replaced with a map of Crete and drop-down, detailed overlays of Agios Nikolaos, Heraklion, and Mournies. Ash trays and coffee cups are the only non-essential accessories in a room that hasn't an inch to spare.

Captain Wil Bishop and his nine men arrived in Berlin before Nick and the others touched down from D.C. By the time they'd been assigned to the transient barracks at Berlin Brigade, the flight from D.C., via London, had landed. Their orders were to proceed from Brigade directly to the Zehlendorf office in pairs so as not to draw too much attention. Dressed in civvies, all ten arrived within 30 minutes of each other. That was six hours ago, enough time to cover the mission's essentials.

The team's next stop is Tempelhof to check on the equipment sortie due in less than an hour. Nick takes the opportunity to review the broad outlines of their mission.

"A sniper team at Souda and Agios Nikolaos will confirm the landings. We'll give the Russians less than 2 minutes from deployment before we take out their beach security. They should leave two men per craft, a total of eight men on each beach. We take out the radio man first. If they leave him on the beach he'll be carrying an R-129 which should make him easy to spot. At Agios Nikolaos, we'll have moved the politicos and drawn the Russians into the hotel. Our best estimate is that they'll deploy no more than 12 into the hotel. Anything more than that will be unworkable due to the tight spaces. That means as many as 22 men in the streets to cover the hotel team. Again, once they realize the hotel is empty, they might stand down. We'll have ten men on buildings near the hotel covering most of the hotel's perimeter. If we can't empty the hotel, whoever's in there is going to take a beating."

"Nick. Sorry to interrupt, but something just occurred to me."

"What's that, Captain?"

"What if the team's a demolition rather than extraction team? What if the Russians are just going to blow up the hotel killing everyone in it rather than bother with kidnapping the big shots?"

"We'll know as soon as they reach the hotel. If they're going to blow it, they'll start setting charges immediately. In that case, we've got a firefight on our hands. We can't let them blow that hotel. Even if our guys are out, the Greeks are going to think their politicians are dead, and with a Russian warship sitting a mile of the coast, all hell is going to break loose. Bottom line, we can't let them blow the hotel."

CHAPTER 54

CLEAR STATIC

Communications specialist Ben Sacolick knocks on the room's threshold and pokes his head in.

"Nick, I've got Bob Arnold on secure comms. He says it's urgent."

"Excuse me, gentlemen."

Nick follows Sacolick back into the comms room.

"Line 4."

"Thanks, Ben."

Nick pushes the phone's flashing button and picks up the receiver.

"Bob, Nick here. What can I do for you?"

"Some strange shit going on here, Nick."

"How's that?"

"We're getting some hits in the clear from Moscow about Crete."

"More confirmation. Sounds good."

"Not really. It's back channel traffic, and it looks like it's aimed squarely at us."

"They're leaking their own operation?" Nick is incredulous.

"It's a set up; someone's trying to roll Krushchev. Thinks he'll cave if the Americans flex their muscles. Inside Politburo shit. They're dribbling it out to Defense. Not too subtle. A Pentagon staffer got ahold of it and now the Joint Chiefs are sniffing around. I got it from a contact at Defense."

"Maybe the President should tell them to back the fuck off."

"It's not that simple, Nick."

"Where's the Director on this?"

"I just got off the phone with him. He's mad as hell, but he's hanging in there for now. He doesn't like being whipsawed by Russians, Pentagon brass, or anyone else."

"So what's the upshot here?"

"Tough to say at this point. You're still a go, but my guess is we'll be on high alert status on April 30th, and if your op goes sour, Uncle Sam is going to be ready to pull the trigger. Acquiescing to a new set of realities in the Eastern Med after the fact, which was never an attractive option, is no longer in the picture."

"So there's no breathing room."

"None."

"Okay, Bob. Thanks for the heads up."

"Thought you should know. Out here."

Nick hangs up as Ben Sacolick disconnects the secure line. Ted Durant walks in from the war room.

"Anything else for the men, Nick?"

"Sure, Ted. Thanks."

Ted and Nick go back into the war room. The men are looking over the maps and diagrams, chatting, and exchanging impressions about the mission. The mood in the room is professional and upbeat.

"Gentlemen, if I could have your attention for just a moment."

They break off their conversations.

"That was Bob Arnold at CIA in D.C. Without going into the details, his message is that we're absolutely in a no-fail posture, no doubt about it."

"Only way we operate, Nick," is Captain Bishop's immediate response.

"Not a problem, Nick. Let's get back to work," Bill Johnson offers.

"All right, then. Let's get to Tempelhof for an equipment check. We've got about six more hours of work before we can call it a day."

CHAPTER 55

THE HARDWARE STORE

The hangar at Tempelhof is closely guarded by a dozen Air Police from the 7350th Air Base Squadron. Two M-38A1 Jeeps and three pallets of equipment inside the hangar arrived via a Douglass C-124 Globemaster while Nick was briefing the men from the 10th Special Forces Group. The Jeeps and the materiel on the pallets were requisitioned by the Director after green-lighting the mission and now need to be logged, inspected, and tested. The operation is designed for maximum effect with minimum hardware. Equipment redundancy is not feasible. Whatever the men bring with them must be in perfect working order.

Inspecting, tuning, on-road and off-road testing, and maintaining the Jeeps will be the job of Sergeant Jim Mikan, a transportation specialist with the 10th Special Forces Group. The rest of the men will break out the three pallets of materiel while items are checked against Nick's manifest.

The men will then inspect each item to the extent possible to ensure its functionality. All M61 grenades and the newly-developed M14 anti-personnel mines will undergo visual inspections. The team will perform comms checks over their AN/PRC-8 ("prick eight") radios to calibrate frequencies and distances; prick-six batteries will be tested to ensure a minimum 4-hour life; Nash-Kelvinator M3 binoculars and M82 sniper scopes will be tested against known distances for precision. The light arms–M1911 side arms, M1928 Thompson submachine guns, M1C sniper rifles, and M7A3 grenade launchers–will be tested extensively at Berlin Brigade's firing and grenade ranges. All sights and scopes will be zeroed at the ranges for their intended users.

The men methodically unload, inventory and begin checking the materiel. Given the precision of the tasks and the amount of equipment, they will likely be working well past midnight. Nick knows the long day is not a problem. He knows that none of them will give any thought to the sacrifices expected of them over the next few weeks of briefings, training, and live mission. Because he knows that in all the combined years of service these men have given to their country, not one of them has ever placed himself ahead of the mission.

CHAPTER 56

FILLING A GAP

"Terry, let me know when Arnie gets in."

"He's already here."

"Sorry. Can you tell him I need to see him?"

"Right away, Mr. Temple."

While Nick waits for Arnie, he goes over the timetable the team has established for getting themselves and their equipment onto Crete. If they arrive too soon, news of their arrival will flood the small island putting the mission in jeopardy. If they wait until the last minute, unexpected contingencies as simple as the weather and as complex as local police or military interference could mean the Russian operation goes down unopposed. Finding that exact point between the two has been the focus of the team's debate for the last 48 hours.

Nick's concentration is broken by a knock on the door, followed by Arnie Miller's entrance.

"What's up, boss?"

"Have a seat, Arnie. I've got a proposal for you."

"Find a replacement for Mika?"

"Not possible."

"Agreed."

"No. I want you in on the Crete operation. I need someone to work with Vanessa inside the hotel in Agios Nikolaos. One person just isn't enough."

"Let me get this straight. You want me to check into a hotel on the Mediterranean with your girlfriend."

Nick can't help laughing.

"I'm afraid there's more to it than that."

"I was wondering when you'd get around to me. You got an NSA guy, a couple of spooks from across the pond, a Special Forces Team, and the best looking woman in West Berlin, hell maybe in all of Berlin. And I'm asking myself, why not Arnie Miller? Since when does my shit stink?"

"Honestly, I wanted you to run things here during the operation. But I need someone else besides Vanessa inside that hotel. Are you in?"

"Hell yes I'm in. When do we start?"

"Right now. Spend the rest of the day in the war room. The docs you need to review are all up there. Go over our plan with a critical eye, and not just the part involving you. If you think we've left anything out, made unsupportable assumptions, failed to account for anything, I need to know. In the meantime, focus on what Vanessa will be doing in the hotel. Where you see her name, add yours. And don't be shy on the critique. The more eyes we get on this thing the better."

"Consider it done. Let's talk tomorrow morning."

"Perfect."

Arnie gets up to leave. As he heads out the door Nick stops him.

"Arnie."

"What's that boss?"

"Glad to have you on board. And I'm sorry I didn't ask you earlier."

"No sweat. But don't expect a kiss. I'm not your type."

They both laugh as Arnie leaves the office, closing the door behind him. The addition of Arnie to the team allays some of Nick's worries about Vanessa. At the same time, another close friend will now be in harm's way, but that's the business they're both in.

CHAPTER 57

THE FRONT DOOR

Nick and Arnie Miller step off TAE Greek National Airlines flight 57 from Athens shortly after noon on Monday, April 25, 1955. Having cleared customs during their brief layover in Athens they collect their baggage immediately. Nick, as has become his habit, has a large stash of American dollars in his flight bag's false bottom. That the bag has made it thus far undetected on a number of trips through Greek customs is a source of some amazement to him. It may explain why the Soviets are feeling confident that Crete will be easy pickings. Sometimes Nick is of half a mind to let the Russians take over Crete. The West can then sit back and watch the Soviets get ground down and slowly bled to death by an island population bristling with the memories of an atrocious Nazi occupation. The risk, however slight, of eventual Soviet conquest and domination, or, at the very least, a Cretan socialist puppet state doing the bidding of their masters in the Kremlin, is too great to allow it to happen without a fight. The bell is about to ring; Nick and his small team will have to answer.

They gather their baggage and head for the taxi stand just outside of the airport's modest lounge. Arnie's destination is the Phoenician Hotel in Agios Nikolaos, the hotel that will be home to Crete's Governor-General and its four Prefects five days from now. Vanessa will arrive in two days.

Nick catches a ride to a hotel off Lions Square in the heart of Heraklion. The number of hotels built since 1950, the year tourism began to spread on the island, makes it possible for these two Americans to enter and stay on Crete for their brief visit in virtual anonymity. Ted Durant, no more than 24 hours behind them, will check in to a hotel situated at the edge of Heraklion's harbor a day before his radio intercept and transmission equipment arrives with the men from the 10th Special Forces Group. Kyle Richardson and Bill Johnson are due in tonight. They'll rendezvous with Nick in front of the Venetian Loggia at 2200 hours local time to coordinate any last minute operational adjustments.

Two days from now all of the pieces will be in place.

CHAPTER 58

EARLY BIRDS

The town of Ierapetra on the Libyan Sea is due south of Agios Nikolaos. The distance between the two towns is no more than 20 miles as the crow flies, but the rugged terrain between the two means any trip from one town to the other is a slow, meandering journey that can take four hours or more, depending on what else is on the road. Because of the terrain, there is no direct route between the two towns. The main road out of Ierapetra runs northeast through a valley to Pachia Ammos at the southern end of Mirabello Bay. From there, travelers turn west and follow the wrap of the bay for about eight miles to Agios Nikolaos. The road is narrow, treacherous, and carved into mountains that spill into the sea. The geographic separation between Ierapetra and Agios Nikolaos makes the Libyan Sea town a perfect anonymous point of entry for the men on Nick's team from the 10th Special Forces Group.

They–men, materiel, and the team's two Jeeps–take a hop from Berlin to Istanbul, and from there to Tel Aviv. From Tel Aviv they travel north to the port at Haifa courtesy of the Israeli Army where they board a small freighter out of Panama for the more than 500 mile trip to Crete. Ten miles off of the coast of Ierapetra, the freighter and its passengers rendezvous with two Sicilian fishing boats hired with no small difficulty before the team left Berlin. The fishing boats' owner, Giovanni Chinnici, provided advance intelligence for the 7th Army's invasion of Sicily in 1943, and has been providing services on an as needed basis to various arms of the American government ever since.

Both fishing boats are rigged with a transom that can be dropped for easy offloading with the stern to. The Jeeps, men and gear are loaded onto the two boats using the freighter's cranes. Nearly every available square inch of the boats' decks is used for the operation. Loading takes just under thirty minutes after which the freighter heads back for Haifa and the fishing boats head for Crete. The two sets of men pile their gear and themselves into the Jeep so that the can disembark immediately upon arrival.

They reach Ierapetra a little after 2 a.m. local time at a point along the seawall just north of town that dips down to no more than a foot above high tide. The Jeeps' drivers start the engines. Chinnici, at the helm of the first boat, backs the boat so its stern is against the seawall. The boat's lone crew member drops the transom and ties the two lines from either side of the boat to bollards on the seawall. The Jeep, its cargo, and its men, drive immediately onto the wharf. As soon as Chinnici's boat clears the landing, the other boat repeats the maneuver, offloading its cargo less than a minute after landing.

The small, undetected American invasion of Crete begins, with an assist from an old, reliable ally, as ten men and their gear drive off into the night in search of the narrow valley road to Pachia Ammos. They'll travel together to an abandoned chapel just south of Agios Nikolaos where they'll spend the next 20 hours. At midnight, three of the men–Captain Wil Bishop, Kyle Richardson, and Bill Johnson–will leave the chapel and continue on to Mournies. At that point, both teams will be in place to respond to the Russian commando Strike Teams headed their way.

CHAPTER 59

MEANWHILE, BACK AT THE RANCH

The Director pushes a button on his desk intercom.

"Cheryl, tell Bob Arnold I want him in my office as fast as his old legs will get him here."

A response from his secretary comes over the Director's speaker.

"He's standing right here. Should I send him in, sir?"

"Damn right!"

Bob Arnold enters the Director's office without knocking. Even though his superior is clearly angry, Arnold is calm and collected as he sits down.

"Nice timing, I'd say," Bob offers.

"Well I've got a thing or two to say about timing."

The Director waves a letter he's holding in his right hand in Arnold's general direction.

"Did you know about this?"

"You're going to have be more specific, sir."

"Temple's shacking up with a double agent. That specific enough for you?"

"Yes."

"Yes what?"

"Yes, I knew about it. I got a call from his wife a while back."

"Jesus H. Christ! I've got about a thousand goddam spies working for me and I have to find out from his wife that the spy I trusted to stop the Commies from taking over the Mediterranean is playing hide the salami with some Nazi widow, a double agent! From his wife!"

"She's not a double agent."

"Oh no? Then what was she doing with Vasily Malenkov before our boy Nick hopped aboard?"

"Getting information for us. Strictly volunteer. By all accounts she's a remarkable woman."

"By all accounts, she's not his wife. By all accounts, he's still married. By all accounts, she was married to a Wehrmacht officer and has slept with a KGB operations chief. So don't give me that 'by all accounts' bullshit. Damn it, Bob. Why wasn't I told about this? Jesus, if this goes beyond this office, the whole operation is in jeopardy. It may already be. I'm not sure I can afford to have him leading up this effort. If this thing goes south someone's going to put the pieces together and then it's really going to hit the fan. We won't get a dime from Congress for a decade. We'll be essentially out of business."

"Want some advice?"

"I don't know. Why should I listen to you, or anyone else from the damn crew that kept this thing from me?"

"Because I'm the only one in this building with the nerve to tell it like it is. Here's the advice: get off your high horse and stay out of the way of the operation. The damn crew, as you call us, just happened to figure out the biggest move by the Commies since Mao grabbed China. And one of the members of the damn crew is sitting on Crete right now about to go toe to toe with about the toughest bunch of Commies they've ever produced over there in Commie land. And there's a better than even chance that the next time you see that member of the damn crew will be when you're looking at a picture of his dead body rotting in some rat hole of a morgue half way around the world. So what if he's banging a piece of German tail who, by the way, is also on Crete risking her life for our country, not hers, ours. That's why you should listen to me and that's my advice all wrapped up for you. If you can't see that's the right thing to do then maybe one of us should get a new job."

By the time Bob Arnold finishes the Director has managed to cool down enough to think rationally about what his choices are. In short, he knows he's stuck with Nick Temple, for better or worse.

"You know as well as I do that at this point I've got to let the operation proceed with Temple as planned. And you also know that if this thing turns into a mess the only detail anyone will focus on is Vanessa Porter's presence smack dab in the middle of the whole shooting match."

The Director and Bob Arnold silently and simultaneously contemplate the unthinkable – what their world will look like if the mission fails. Once again, the Director speaks up.

"I've been getting Nick's reports, but I'm not sending anything his way. When Durant gets set up down there, you let Nick know that the moment Crete is secure he needs to get Porter to Berlin and himself to this office so I can figure out what future, if any, he has."

"You think it's a good idea to relay that message at this point?"

"I don't think it'll do any harm, and it just might be the motivation he needs in any tight spot over the next 72 hours."

"All right, then. I'll send the message."

Bob stands to leave.

"Anything else I should know, Bob?"

"No, sir. That covers it. And I owe you an apology. I just couldn't bring myself to rat him out."

"Apology accepted. Let's get back to work"

Both men, with the security of the West and the safety of their countrymen 5300 miles away weighing heavily on their minds, return to the unsatisfying business of waiting.

CHAPTER 60

GOTCHA!

Ted Durant scans the airwaves for Black Sea Fleet communications. He sits at a makeshift intercept position in his 3ʳᵈ floor room at the Ulysses Hotel built at the edge of Heraklion's harbor. His AN/GRR-5 field receiver, called an "angry five" by seasoned ops, was delivered shortly before dawn by two men from the Special Forces Group Team that landed in Ierapetra less than 24 hours ago. Since getting the receiver up and running he's been searching non-stop for any traffic coming from the north side of the island. If the Russians are parked in the Libyan Sea, he won't hear a thing. If they're north, in the Aegean, he might get lucky.

Nothing of note for more than five hours. Some civilian freighter chatter, a few weather reports, some local police traffic, a few transmissions from the airport's control tower, and that's about it. After more than five hours of non-stop spinning the receiver's dial up and down the frequency range, he rolls across a faint signal carrying Russian voice in the clear. He presses on his headphones to block out all other noise. Atmospherics are stepping on the signal big time, but after a few tries he has it dialed in.

He's picking up two voices, one a native Russian speaker, the other heavily accented Russian, probably a Greek. They're making his job easy by transmitting and receiving both sides of the conversation on the same frequency. At first the transmissions are nothing more than comms checks – an exchange of call signs followed by "Ponyal," the

Russian equivalent of "I read you." Both radios are push-to-talk–lots of static when they come up–and one of them is closer to Heraklion, its signal stronger than the other.

One op, the Greek, lets the other one know he's ready to receive – "K priyomu gotov!" Groups of numbers start coming from the Russian immediately. Durant hasn't taken hand copy in a while, but he's able to keep up as groups of four-fig are transmitted. He immediately sees the pattern: five groups of four-figure encryption. He gets it all down–20 sets in all–wondering whether he has it right, and then he catches a break.

"Ne ponyal. Povtari!" The Greek lost the signal at some point and has to ask for the transmission to be repeated.

The second time through is slower, clearer, and Durant is sure he has it. On this pass, knowing the pattern, he copies the figures in columns of five.

"Konets." The end. The numbers stop. The signal goes down.

Durant immediately compares the 20 lines of five sets of four-fig in the second pass to make sure they're identical with those in the first pass. Once certain the two sets are identical, he pulls his code book out of his flight bag to see if he can break out the numbers. He keeps his headphones on in case the ops come back up.

The first two lines looks like the key he pulled out of transmissions to the forward area from Moscow to inform commanders of Stalin's death back in '53. The intercepts were solid, and once he knew what he was looking for–instructions to the Soviet Army about their posture in the immediate aftermath of the death of their brutal leader–the rest was relatively easy. He works the four-fig through his handwritten code book, finds the key and, using the code's algorithm, breaks out the rest of the transmission. He'll know immediately if he's on the right track.

After the key lines, the next four lines should be an event and a date, or rather a day: "signal" ("A nice, easy cognate" Durant thinks to himself), and "Poslezavtra" (the day after tomorrow). If he has the key right, the next two lines should be a time. They are: "Polnoch'" (midnight). If the key holds, the next four lines should be a loc. Again, they are: "Ostrov vsekh Svyatykh (the Island of All Saints). With eight lines left, the transmission repeats the words "tri raza" (three times) until the final line which breaks out to read "Konets" (end). Pay dirt!

Durant checks his work again, grabs the map of Crete off his bed and pulls it to him. Scanning the north coast of Crete he sees it! Agioi Pantes, the Island of All Saints. Someone, probably the Greek op, will signal the commandos three times from the Island of All Saints two days from today at midnight. It's a lock: standard Soviet four-fig with an identified key leaving no doubts.

He has to get the information to the rest of the team. Nick has scheduled a radio comms check for 1430 hours local time, 20 minutes from now. He fires up the AN/PRC-8 so he'll be ready the moment 1430 rolls around.

As Ted Durant checks his work one last time he allows his mind to contemplate the effect of the intercept. It's simple: if they can interrupt the signal coming from the Island of All Saints, interrupt it in a way that lets the Soviets know they're in for a fight, the commandos will know they've lost the element of surprise and maybe, just maybe stand down the entire reckless operation before the serious bloodshed starts.

CHAPTER 61

SEVEN'S A CROWD

All of the rooms, and there are only five of them, on the second floor of the Phoenician Hotel in Agios Nikolaos look out onto Mirabello Bay. Arnie Miller sits in a room at the north end of the floor. Vanessa Porter does the same at the other end of the hall. Between their rooms are the remaining three, the middle of which is occupied by Crete's Governor-General. The other two rooms each contain two of Crete's Prefects. The heart of Crete's government is in three rooms in a small hotel; the heart of Crete's government is far more vulnerable than the men who comprise that heart imagine.

At precisely eleven o'clock at night, Arnie and Vanessa leave their rooms and head for the Governor-General's room. As agreed, Vanessa knocks.

"Ti esti; (Who is it?)"

"A friend," is Vanessa's muted response.

She waits.

The Governor-General, a stout and slightly formal man in his early fifties, opens the door.

Vanessa steps aside. Arnie, M119 semiautomatic drawn, swings to face the Governor-General.

"Back in the room. Go, go, go!" Arnie orders.

The Governor-General, wide-eyed with alarm, complies. Arnie follows him into the room. Vanessa, close behind, shuts and locks the door behind them.

"Who are you? What is this outrage? Are you thieves? Do you know who I am?"

Arnie takes over.

"Take it easy, pops. We're on your side."

While keeping the Governor-General covered, Miller pulls out his CIA identification.

"The Russians are going to be here in about an hour. They're going to kill you and your four friends, and then they're going to take over your island. If that's okay with you, let me know, and I'll be on my way."

"This is an outrage! How dare you meddle in the internal affairs of a sovereign nation!"

"Maybe you didn't understand, so I'll repeat. This is no internal affair. Unless you and the Prefects do as I say, you'll be dead in an hour and Crete will be a satellite of the Soviet Union by noon tomorrow."

"I don't believe you. This is some ridiculous scheme. Are you here to rob me? Then rob me, but don't continue this bizarre charade."

Arnie decides it's time to break out the big guns. He pulls an envelope from his back pocket addressed to the Governor-General. It's a personal note from the President of the United States confirming Arnie's claim of the danger of imminent takeover. It was the Director's idea, and a good one at that.

As the Governor-General reads the note, he begins to understand his vulnerability. He slumps down on the room's bed, and runs his hand through his hair. He seems lost in thought.

"Sir, I realize this must come as quite a shock to you, but we don't have a lot of time. Our orders are to evacuate you and the Prefects from the hotel. We'll need your assistance with the others."

"What should I call you?"

"My apologies. I'm Arnold Miller, and this is Mrs. Vanessa Porter. And you have to believe me. We're here to help."

"Well Mr. Miller and Mrs. Porter, it appears that I'm at your mercy."

"Mr. Governor-General. We are at your service. Now, if you'll come with me."

Arnie, Vanessa, and Crete's Governor-General leave the small hotel room to gather the four prefects. If all goes according to plan the heart of Crete's government will be safely ensconced in a Heraklion hotel with Arnie Miller as their unofficial host in less than an hour. And Vanessa Porter will be back in Agios Nikolaos to provide whatever real time intel she can from inside the Phoenician Hotel.

CHAPTER 62

BACK TO THE BEGINNING

The kill was easy. Ted Durant's intel was spot on. The Soviets' signalman is dead. The single shot from Nick's rifle causes a few lights in town to come on, but the quick return of absolute silence ends the brief inquiry of the curious Greeks.

Nick is tempted to stay put, to see if the Russians realize they've lost the element of surprise and stand down the raid. But he has to move. If the assault is still a go, Nick needs to shift his position to gain a better sweep of the landing zone – the beach just north of Agios Nikolaos. He shoulders his weapon and silently shimmies down the roof's drainpipe on the back of the building. His objective, a two-story building housing a harbor restaurant four blocks away.

As he moves silently through the narrow streets of the small town he picks up the distant sound of outboard motors on Mirabello Bay headed his way. The Russians are once again sending men into a cauldron of slaughter.

"Some things never change," Nick thinks to himself.

Captain Shevardnadze terminates the radio transmission. The order from the Black Sea Fleet command is clear. The death of the signalman changes nothing about the plan of attack. There is no turning back.

CHAPTER 63

BONFIRES ON THE BEACHES

Three inflatable craft loaded with Russian Spetsnaz GRU commandos and their gear approach the beach at Agios Nikolaos within seconds of each other, their way lighted by a nearly full moon. The craft are approximately 50 meters apart. The helmsman in each boat cuts the outboard engine. Ten men, dressed from head to foot in black, jump out of each inflatable. Three men on each side grab straps on the boat's pontoons and run the inflatables another 20 meters beyond the high tide mark on the beach. The other four men from each craft deploy to protect the rear and the flanks of the landing party just beyond the edge of the slight surf.

Once the craft are in place, 24 men, eight from each boat, move swiftly and steadily forward off the beach onto the road that separates the town from the beach. The remaining six men, each on one knee with his weapon in a firing posture, guard the inflatables and their fellow commandos' escape route.

Nick is impressed as he watches the precision landing and deployment from his perch two stories up. His new position puts the entire beach easily within range.

"Where's the fourth boat?" he thinks to himself.

He scans the beach with his binoculars again to see if he can pick up the missing boat.

"Nothing. Three boats. Is the fourth boat at another location? Too late to do anything about it now."

He scans the beach again to see if he can identify the team's radio operator. Third one in, range of no more than 150 meters. The rest of the team has scattered into town and will shortly be nearly a quarter mile from the beach.

Nick puts down his binoculars and picks up his PRC-6 radio.

"Team Alpha, this is Big Dog. Ivan's off the beach. Out."

He puts down the radio and picks up his rifle. Through the scope he can see the radio operator hasn't moved. Nick zeroes in, exhales, and squeezes the trigger. The report from the rifle sounds like lightning against the still of the night. The radio operator drops immediately. Nick turns to the next commando up the beach, aims and fires. Two down, four to go. By now the remaining four are scrambling for cover towards the coast road. One returns a harmless three-round burst of automatic fire from his AK-47 in Nick's general direction. Nick scans his sector once again. He sees one of the commandos moving back towards the water.

"He's trying to get the radio," Nick realizes.

Nick picks up the dead radio operator through his scope. He's face down in on the beach, the radio strapped to his inert back. Before his comrade can retrieve the radio, Nick pumps two rounds into the R-129 rendering it useless. Another burst of fire comes from the beach, but they haven't got a lock on him so the rounds strike nowhere near Nick's position.

Four shots, two dead, comms disabled, less than sixty seconds. So far, so good, but Nick knows staying on the roof any longer would be pushing it. Through his scope he sees one of the commandos signal to two others to deploy in Nick's direction. Time to move again.

Nick leaves the M1C rifle and its scope in place, slings his PRC-6 over his shoulder, and heads over to the edge of the flat roof. He eases himself over the side, clings to the roof dangling no more than four feet above an outdoor landing and drops down without a sound. He scrambles down the outer staircase to join the rest of his team surrounding the hotel. The Russians should be getting to the hotel within the next sixty seconds.

It's just past midnight, and the beach at Souda well west of Heraklion is quiet after the landing. Twenty-four of the Soviet Union's commandos, the best Mother Russia can put in the field, double-time for the Naval Communications station at Mournies while six men remain on the beach, guarding the landing craft and the Strike Team's eventual retreat. The moonlight increases their vulnerability; the loss of surprise made clear by the signalman's death moves defeat way up on the list of probable outcomes. But there will be no change to the assault plan: secure the beach, surround the radio station, suppress any opposition, take control of the station, and begin transmitting over the civilian airwaves the news of Crete's glorious socialist revolution.

The first wrinkle in the plan comes from the rifle of Captain Wil Bishop. Once the main body of the assault force is at least half a mile in from the coast, Bishop, who watched the entire landing from a patch of scrubby vegetation near an access road at the south end of the beach, drops the radioman and quickly picks off two more from the rear guard.

Without waiting to see if the surviving men return fire, Bishop scrambles from his position to join the team's remaining two men two blocks away from the radio station. The surprise they have waiting for the Soviets should rival the pending May Day celebrations back in Moscow. The odds are still long–24 of the Soviet Union's best against three Americans–but the plastique that will soon obliterate the building housing the Greek Navy's radio transmission station should even things up nicely.

CHAPTER 64

THE MEAN STREETS

On a narrow street in Agios Nikolaos, Yuri Shevardnadze hears the report of a sniper's rifle from nearly half a mile away. His worst fear, that they lost the critical element of surprise when the signalman was assassinated, is now confirmed as a deadly reality. The same thought is surely racing through the mind of each man on the team. Shevardnadze knows his dreams of glory will be purchased, if at all, at a staggering cost. The last minute command decision to reduce the assault force to thirty men at each location will, if nothing else, cut their losses. With no time for recon, and no time to improvise, he and his men resolutely deploy to their prearranged positions around the small Phoenician Hotel. To bolster his considerable courage, he carries the battle cry of the defenders of Stalingrad in his heart – Ni Shagu Nazad! Not a step backward!

Captain Bishop and his men settle into positions two blocks above the radio station. Bishop is at the south end of the block perched on a small flat roof of a one story house. The roof is accessible from the steep hillside just behind it. His fellow team members, Kyle Richardson and Bill Johnson, are on a similar small building at the north end of the block. From the two vantage points they have a perfect view of the advancing Spetsnaz Strike Team moving rapidly towards their target.

Six men at the tip of the Strike Team's spear surround the radio station building to provide security and suppressing fire for the others. A second group of six places itself, three on each side, at the building's front entrance in its west wall clearly in view of Bishop and his men. A third group of six scrambles to the rear entrance, while the final group of six guards the team's rear flank.

"These guys are good. Quick, precise, thorough. Too bad they're all going to die," Bishop thinks to himself. Once he is certain that the maximum number of men are within the kill radius, he picks up his radio.

"Okay. Blow it."

"Roger, out," is the instant response from Richardson.

Bishop turns his back to the radio station to shield his eyes from the flash. He waits . . . five seconds . . . ten seconds . . . fifteen seconds . . . nothing!

"We have a major malfunction," is the next transmission from Richardson. Without hesitating, Bishop responds.

"Wait for my signal."

Captain Bishop runs to the back of the building, jumps off the roof and hits the steep hillside slope running. He sprints into the street and towards the north end of the block. He has to check the transmission line from one end to the other, and they've got to blow that building even if it means getting right in Ivan's face.

He reaches the wire just below Richardson and Johnson's position, follows it across the street and down an alley that leads to the station. As he gets to the next block he sees the break – maybe a cart, maybe even a footstep, but not a deliberate cut. That's the good news. The bad news is that as he kneels down to splice the break he catches motion out of the corner of his eye. Instinctively he dives for the safety and darkness of a doorway. A shot rings out, two more! They've spotted him!

He gets on his radio.

"Pour it on! Pour it on! One o'clock from your position, one block east. Do it!"

A fury of automatic weapons fire lights up the night, every third round a blazing tracer. Rounds slam into plaster walls, and in no time the street is a deafening and deadly mess of flying plaster, dust, and tracer rounds.

The Soviets dive for cover and return fire. Bishop needs no more than 10 seconds at the break, but he's not going to get it with small arms fire.

He grabs an M61 hand grenade from a metal loop on his web gear, pulls the pin, steps out of the doorway and lets it fly. He takes cover in the doorway. The blast from the grenade sends debris flying by him. There's a brief silence from the Soviet position as the survivors recover from the grenade blast. Now's his chance!

He dives for the break, grabs both ends of the wire, and quickly twists a splice. He finishes and turns just as a round from an AK-47 slams into his lower back. His legs are instantly paralyzed. He desperately claws at the cobblestone street and drags himself to the safety of the doorway. Although he has no feeling in his legs, the pain in his lower back burns like nothing he has ever felt. In spite of the pain, he grabs for the Thompson submachine gun strapped to his shoulder.

Three members of the Strike Team lie dead in the street from Bishop's grenade. Six of the Soviets enter the radio station after shattering its back door. The surviving men at the front are pinned down by the hail of gunfire from Bishop's two men. Three other commandos begin to close on Bishop's position.

"Blow it now!" Captain Bishop screams into his radio.

"Get out of there, Captain," is the response.

"No time! Blow it!"

Automatic fire seems to come from all directions as the Soviets corner Bishop. Rounds start slamming into him. Time almost stops as he sees his body being slowly ripped to shreds. Just as he is about to lose consciousness and his life, he hears the sudden and startling roar of an explosion that destroys the radio station and anyone in or near it. Bishop, smiling at the instant of his death, falls face first into the street, his last second on earth redeemed in victory.

Shevardnadze's Strike Team, winding its way through the streets of Agios Nikolaos, has no idea that half of the assault plan is about to go up in a tremendous blast. The distance between the two prongs of the attack makes communication impossible. The plan, coordinated by men much more comfortable with throwing an infantry division into the line than with small unit tactics, is starting to reveal its weaknesses.

Shevardnadze's men, silently approaching the Phoenician Hotel, are carefully watched by Temple and his group who surround the hotel from various vantage points no more than 100 meters away. Vanessa remains inside with two Prefects who refused to evacuate with Arnie Miller. She guards them, knowing she may have to kill them rather than let them be taken by the Soviets. Nick is resolute. No Spetsnaz commando will enter the hotel.

The commandos pause. Nick looks up from his binoculars, searching for any sort of signal that would have caused the commandos to halt. And then he sees it! Not a signal, but the plan. Satchels start coming off the backs of at least half the men in the groups. The Soviets have no intention of entering the hotel; their orders are to blow it up! Judging by the amount of plastique now visible, their orders are to reduce it to rubble to leave the impression that the heads of Crete's government are no more.

Nick gets on the radio.

"Team Alpha, this is Big Dog. They're going to blow it."

"Roger, Big Dog. We're on it."

The possibility is one they'd considered and rehearsed for while training in Berlin. They knew then, and Nick knows now, that they're looking at a bloodbath, a good old fashioned door to door firefight until someone surrenders the field. He looks through his binoculars again. Shevardnadze's men have divided the plastique and are headed for the building's structural weak spots. Time's up.

Nick gets back on the radio.

"On my mark, boys."

Nick doesn't wait for a response. He fires a three-round burst from his Thomson submachine gun. A commando drops. Twelve of

Shevardnadze's men immediately take positions to cover the actions of the demolition teams who continue to place their explosives with expert precision. Suddenly the air is full of small arms fire. Nick's men all understand that they cannot allow the building to be destroyed. As they fire, they maneuver through the streets of Agios Nikolaos to engage their targets. Soon the two sides firing at each other are no more than 50 meters apart.

Vanessa knows she has to get the two recalcitrant Prefects out of the hotel as soon as the shooting starts. The intensity of the firefight tells her the Russians are determined to destroy rather than storm the hotel. She points her M119 .45 caliber pistol at the two men.

"Gentlemen. We must leave. There's a car waiting at the hotel's service entrance. Drive to the Ulysses Hotel in Heraklion. Do you know it?"

"Of course," is the answer of the older of the two Prefects.

"Go to the room of Ted Durant. You'll be safe there. Do you understand?"

"Yes, of course."

"We'll take the stairwell at the north end of the hallway. The service entrance is just beyond the door at the bottom of the stairwell. As you can hear, your cooperation may mean the difference between life and death for you, me, and all of Crete. It's time for us to go."

She motions for them to follow her out of the room. They walk briskly to the stairwell. The gun battle just outside the hotel rages fiercely. They get to the bottom of the stairwell and walk five paces down the hallway until they reach the service entrance. Vanessa motions for them to stop. The two men, terrified by the sounds of deadly combat raging around them, do as they're told.

Vanessa cracks the door open to see if they'll be stepping into anyone's line of fire. As soon as she ascertains that the firing is a relatively safe distance on the other side of the hotel, she opens the door all the way and motions to the two men. As she told them, a car sits on the narrow street behind the hotel.

"The keys are in it. Drive west, up above the town first. If you go straight out, you'll certainly be shot. Remember, Ulysses Hotel, Ted Durant. Now go!"

The two men, frightened but certain that Vanessa's instructions are their only hope of surviving the night, run to the car, jump in, start it and drive away, taking an alley leading west away from the shooting.

As soon as the car is out of sight, Vanessa lets the hotel door close behind her and heads in the direction of the position of Nick and his men.

As the dust from the recently destroyed radio station begins to cover several square blocks of Mournies, Kyle Richardson and Bill Johnson prepare to evacuate. But they're not leaving without Bishop. Having failed to raise him on the radio, they retrace the route of the detonation wire they laid. Richardson sees him first.

They both sprint to Bishop's body. They check for signs of life, but even a blind man could see that Bishop is dead. Neither man has to express what they both feel deep in their bones. They won't leave their fallen comrade on the battlefield. After quickly removing his gear to lighten the load, Richardson grabs Bishop's lifeless form under the armpits, and Johnson grabs the dead man's boots.

The wail of a siren suddenly pierces the night air.

"Let's get the hell out of here," Johnson declares.

In under two minutes they are driving away from Mournies in a Jeep with their dead commander's body across the back bench. Their destination is Ierapetra where Giovanni Chinnici sits off the coast in his fishing boat ready to pull the three men off the island.

The firefight is producing desired results. The Spetsnaz demolition teams are decimated, but the firing continues as the battle in Agios Nikolaos has become a war of attrition. Nick considers withdrawing, but he is certain that if he does the surviving Soviets will take another crack at blowing the building. Slowly, methodically, Nick and his men close in on the survivors.

Nick is now at the south end of the hotel. He scrambles behind the hotel's narrow wall. Most of the firing from his team is coming from the north moving the remaining commandos his way. He takes a quick look around the wall and sees a Soviet, firing his AK-47, and backing directly towards him. Nick steps out from behind the wall and points his Thompson at the Russian.

"Stoy! (Halt!)" Nick commands.

The Russian does as commanded. It is Shevardnadze. With his back still towards Nick, he responds in fluent English.

"Do not think I am going to surrender."

"Your mission's a failure. Take the rest of your men while you can. There's no point in any more fighting. We'll allow you to collect your dead and wounded."

"I will not leave in disgrace."

Nick is certain that the Russian is about to turn to fire, but he can't bring himself to shoot until he does. A muzzle flash in his peripheral vision causes Nick to lose his concentration for a split second. Shevardnadze's instincts and training tell him this is the moment of survival. He drops and starts to turn in a single motion. As he turns to fire on his American captor a shot rings out from the alleyway to his right. A .45 caliber round catches the young Russian Captain square in the temple instantly ending his life.

Nick lets his own weapon down as Vanessa Porter steps out of the shadows, smoke coming from the barrel of her .45. Nick, amazed at her strength, goes over to her.

"I had no choice. He would have killed you. I had no choice."

"I know. That's enough killing. Let's get the hell out of here."

As they slip away, Nick gets on his radio.

"Cease fire. Cease fire."

The Americans stop firing. The Russians, their appalling casualties testifying to their leaders' callous indifference and their own remarkable courage, seize the opportunity to cut their losses.

Both Russians and Americans withdraw from the center of town. The few surviving Soviet commandos are in headlong retreat for the beach, their numbers decimated, their mission having turned into nothing more than senseless slaughter. The Americans gather at a point just south of the beach. They watch from a distance as the Soviets haul as many of their dead and dying comrades as they can to their inflatable craft.

Nick turns to his own men and counts heads. All present and accounted for. They took what the Soviets considered was their distinct advantage, the element of surprise, and turned it on its head.

As the Soviets head for the open sea and the Americans disperse into the night, the residents of Agios Nikolaos are left to clean up after playing unwitting host to a brief, brutal, and deadly slugfest between the two most powerful nations in the world. Nick Temple knows it could have been far, far worse.

CHAPTER 65

GOOD NEWS TRAVELS FAST

"Ted Durant just finished his last transmission sir."

The communications officer tries to hand the transcript of Ted Durant's communique from Heraklion to the Director who leans back in his chair and closes his eyes.

"Just put it on the desk and tell me what it says."

Having been in the dark for the last twelve hours has been almost more than the Director can take. So much is riding on this improbable gamble – 15 men and a German widow to stop an aggressive Soviet thrust. What the hell was he thinking? He is certain the news will be bad, that Durant got off one final transmission before being arrested pending his execution or a lifetime in the gulag courtesy of his new Soviet masters, and that the morning will bring the highest state of tension between the United States and the Soviet Union since the Berlin Airlift.

"Radio station destroyed, Agios Nikolaos secure. Spetsnaz in full retreat. Team dispersed and returning with body of Captain Bishop, only American KIA. Out. Durant."

The Director opens his eyes and exhales. That's it then: takeover averted and nuclear war put off for the time being. All in a day's work.

"Thank you. That'll be all."

The communications officer leaves. The Director flips a switch on his intercom. His secretary, used to working late in times of crisis, responds.

"Sir?"

"Cheryl. I need to talk to the President."

"Good or bad news, if I may ask, sir?"

"We're going to be fine. We lost a good man, but that's the price we pay in this damn business. Let me know when I can speak with him."

"Right away, sir."

"And tell Bob Arnold I need to see him."

"Yes, sir."

The Director flips the intercom switch to off. He opens up his bottom right desk drawer and pulls out two shot glasses and a bottle of bourbon. He pours two shots. As he sits at his desk, he contemplates the enormous power of his office and how much that power depends on the resolve, brains, and courage of so many other people. He raises his glass and silently toasts them all.

CHAPTER 66

DECOMPRESSION

Nick and Vanessa step aboard Chalky White's Grumman G-73 Mallard. White is right behind them.

"Now, let's talk about your fare, shall we?"

Nick reaches into his flight bag and pulls out three bundles of bills, each containing one thousand American dollars.

"Three grand should do it. Santorini's not much more than a milk run."

"By jove, I like working for you Yanks!"

White takes the money and ducks into the cockpit.

As the seaplane heads away from the dock and out of the harbor, Nick turns to Vanessa.

"It's just a week, but it'll have to do."

"Shouldn't we get back to Berlin?"

"According to the Director's last edict, no doubt about it. But the hell with that. Arnie can handle things for a week. Besides, as soon I land I'm going to have to head to D.C. The ass chewing the Director has in mind for me is going to have to wait."

Nick and Vanessa try to put the horrific events of the last 24 hours behind them. They look forward to the next several days. And they both know that their pending week on Santorini could be the last days they will ever spend together.

The plane climbs steadily as Chalky White sets a course due north for Santorini, away from Crete, away from the bloodshed and broken lives, away from another deadly chess match between two careless giants. The plane's passengers are two anonymous Cold War heroes, alone with their thoughts but bound together in a way few men and women can imagine.

THE END

www.ingramcontent.com/pod-product-compliance
Lightning Source LLC
Chambersburg PA
CBHW061137170626
46809CB00003B/886